A. E. Van Vogt is the supreme sf entertainer. For him the story is above all else the thing: propaganda and moral messages are never allowed to get in the way.

His characters travel through a cosmos of fantastic confusion sustained only by the conviction that within them are undreamed-of powers that they will eventually master.

Destination: Universe! drives a shipload of humans along at a breathless pace, event following event in the style of the old silent picture cliffhangers, to a final destination—and destiny—that will keep the reader spellbound.

"Van Vogt's plots are always ingenious and his action fast"

Edmund Cooper in *The Sunday Times*

Destination: Universe!

A. E. Van Vogt

A JOVE/HBJ BOOK

First Jove/HBJ edition published September 1977

Printed in the United States of America

Jove/HBJ books are published by Jove Publications, Inc.
(Harcourt Brace Jovanovich) 757 Third Avenue, New York,
N.Y. 10017

Contents

Introduction

To my readers:

SCIENCE FICTION is a field of writing where, month after month, every printed word implies to hundreds of thousands of people: "There is change. Look, today's fantastic story is tomorrow's fact."

I admit we authors missed some of the main streams of scientific development. Science fiction writers were woefully unimaginative in predicting the work that was being done even as they wrote their stories. But, after all, a few score of writers turn out about eighty per cent of the science fiction that is printed. They are outnumbered thousands to one by scientists doing research.

I don't think the misses or near-misses are important. The hits outnumber them by a great deal. But what really matters is the attitude that is being fostered. Science fiction has helped, and will—I am sure—continue to help form the forward-looking attitude. It has fostered and will—again, I feel sure of this—continue to foster the great notion that the universe is an area of endless potentiality. Science fiction, as I personally try to write it, glorifies man and his future.

Man over most of the world is in chains. Everywhere, powerful retrogressive forces are at work to keep him enslaved, or are fashioning new, more binding chains. All the powers of misused positivism are arrayed against him. But he will free himself if scientific knowledge can ever penetrate into his prison.

It may seem arrogant for me to claim that science fiction is the medium best able to infiltrate the individual's instinctive defences against the knowledge that can save him. But I do claim it. Almost without knowing it, the reader will find himself accepting new ideas. He will become familiar with thousands of scientific facts which have slipped past the censor he or she carefully maintains against anything as modern and es-

7

sential as science. He can be rescued because the sugar-coated pill is still the most effective method of breaking down the resistances of the inflexible personality.

A. E. van Vogt.

far centaurus

I WAKENED with a start, and thought: How was Renfrew taking it?

I must have moved physically, for blackness edged with pain closed over me. How long I lay in that agonized faint, I have no means of knowing. My next awareness was of the thrusting of the engines that drove the spaceship.

Slowly this time, consciousness returned. I lay very quiet, feeling the weight of my years of sleep, determined to follow the routine prescribed so long ago by Pelham.

I didn't want to faint again.

I lay there, and I thought: It was silly to have worried about Jim Renfrew. He wasn't due to come out of his state of suspended animation for another fifty years.

I began to watch the illuminated face of the clock in the ceiling. It had registered 23:12; now it was 23:22. The ten minutes Pelham had suggested for a time lapse between passivity and initial action was up.

Slowly, I pushed my hand towards the edge of the bed. *Click!* My fingers pressed the button that was there. There was a faint hum. The automatic massager began to fumble gently over my naked form.

First, it rubbed my arms; then it moved to my legs, and so on over my body. As it progressed, I could feel the fine slick of oil that oozed from it working into my dry skin.

A dozen times I could have screamed from the pain of life returning. But in an hour I was able to sit up and turn on the lights.

The small, sparsely furnished, familiar room couldn't hold my attention for more than an instant. I stood up.

The movement must have been too abrupt. I swayed, caught on to the metal column of the bed, and retched discolored stomach juices.

The nausea passed. But it required an effort of will for me

9

to walk to the door, open it, and head along the narrow corridor that led to the control room.

I wasn't supposed to so much as pause there, but a spasm
of absolutely dreadful fascination seized me; and I couldn't
help it. I leaned over the control chair, and glanced at the
chronometer.

It said: 53 years, 7 months, 2 weeks, 0 days, 0 hours and
27 minutes.

Fifty-three years! A little blindly, almost blankly, I
thought: Back on Earth, the people we had known, the
young men we'd gone to college with, that girl who had
kissed me at the party given us the night we left—they were
all dead. Or dying of old age.

I remembered the girl very vividly. She was pretty, viva-
cious, a complete stranger. She had laughed as she offered
her red lips, and said "A kiss for the ugly one, too."

She'd be a grandmother now, or in her grave.

Tears came to my eyes. I brushed them away, and began
to heat the can of concentrated liquid that was to be my first
food. Slowly, my mind calmed.

Fifty-three years and seven and one half months, I thought
drably. Nearly four years over my allotted time. I'd have to
do some figuring before I took another dose of Eternity drug.
Twenty grains had been calculated to preserve my flesh and
my life for exactly fifty years.

The stuff was evidently more potent than Pelham had been
able to estimate from his short period advance tests.

I sat tense, narrow-eyed, thinking about that. Abruptly, I
grew conscious of what I was doing. Laughter spat from my
lips. The sound split the silence like a series of pistol shots,
startling me.

But it also relieved me. Was I sitting here actually being
critical?

A miss of only four years was bull's-eye across that span of
years.

Why, I was alive and still young. Time and space had been
conquered. The universe belonged to man.

I ate my "soup," sipping each spoonful deliberately. I made
the bowl last every second of thirty minutes. Then, greatly refreshed, I made my way back to the control room.

This time I paused for a long look through the plates. It

took only a few moments to locate Sol, a very brightly glowing star in the approximate center of the rear-view plate.

Alpha Centauri required longer to locate. But it shone finally, a glow point in a light-sprinkled darkness.

I wasted no time trying to estimate their distances. They *looked* right. In fifty-one years we had covered approximately one-tenth of the four and one-third light-years to the famous nearest star system.

Satisfied, I threaded my way back to the living quarters. Take them in a row, I thought. Pelham first.

As I opened the air-tight door of Pelham's room, a sickening odor of decayed flesh tingled in my nostrils. With a gasp I slammed the door, stood there in the narrow hallway, shuddering.

After a minute, there was still nothing but the reality.

Pelham was dead.

I cannot clearly remember what I did then. I ran; I know that. I flung open Renfrew's door, then Blake's. The clean, sweet smell of their rooms, the sight of their silent bodies on their beds brought back a measure of my sanity.

A great sadness came to me. Poor, brave Pelham. Inventor of the Eternity drug that had made the great plunge into interstellar space possible, he lay dead now from his own invention.

What was it he had said: "The chances are greatly against any of us dying. But there is what I am calling a death factor of about ten per cent, a by-product of the first dose. If our bodies survive the inital shock, they will survive further doses.

The death factor must be greater than ten percent. That extra four years the drug had kept me asleep—

Gloomily, I went to the storeroom, and procured my personal spacesuit and a tarpaulin. But even with their help it was a horrible business. The drug had preserved the body to some extent, but pieces kept falling off as I lifted it.

At last, I carried the tarpaulin and its contents to the air lock, and shoved it into space.

I felt pressed now for time. These waking periods were to be brief affairs, in which what we called the "current" oxygen was to be used up, but the main reserves were not to be touched. Chemicals in each room slowly refreshed the "current" air over the years, readying it for the next to waken.

In some curious defensive fashion, we had neglected to allow for an emergency like the death of one of our members; even as I climbed out of the spacesuit, I could feel the difference in the air I was breathing.

I went first to the radio. It had been calculated that half a light-year was the limit of radio reception, and we were approaching that limit now.

Hurriedly, though carefully, I wrote my report out, then read it into a transcription record, and started sending. I set the record to repeat a hundred times.

In a little more than five months hence, headlines would be flaring on Earth.

I clamped my written report into the ship log book, and added a note for Renfrew at the bottom. It was a brief tribute to Pelham. My praise was heartfelt, but there was another reason behind my note. They had been pals, Renfrew, the engineering genius who built the ship, and Pelham, the great chemist-doctor, whose Eternity drug had made it possible for men to take this fantastic journey into vastness.

It seemed to me that Renfrew, waking up into the great silence of the hurtling ship, would need my tribute to his friend and colleague. It was little enough for me to do, who loved them both.

The note written, I hastily examined the glowing engines, made notations of several instrument readings, and then counted out fifty-five grains of Eternity drug. That was as close as I could get to the amount I felt would be required for one hundred and fifty years.

For a long moment before sleep came, I thought of Renfrew and the terrible shock that was coming to him on top of all the natural reactions to his situation, that would strike deep into his peculiar, sensitive nature—

I stirred uneasily at the picture.

The worry was still in my mind when darkness came.

Almost instantly, I opened my eyes. I lay thinking: The drug! It hadn't worked.

The draggy feel of my body warned me of the truth. I lay very still watching the clock overhead. This time it was easier to follow the routine except that, once more, I could not refrain from examining the chronometer as I passed through the galley.

It read: 201 years, 1 month, 3 weeks, 5 days, 7 hours, 8 minutes.

I sipped my bowl of that super soup, then went eagerly to the big log book.

It is utterly impossible for me to describe the thrill that coursed through me, as I saw the familiar handwriting of Blake, and then, as I turned back the pages, of Renfrew.

My excitement drained slowly, as I read what Renfrew had written. It was a report; nothing more: gravitometric readings, a careful calculation of the distance covered, a detailed report on the performance of the engines, and, finally, an estimate of our speed variations, based on the seven consistent factors.

It was a splendid mathematical job, a first-rate scientific analysis. But that was all there was. No mention of Pelham, not a word of comment on what I had written or on what had happened.

Renfew had wakened; and if his report was any criterion, he might as well have been a robot.

I knew better than that.

So—I saw as I began to read Blake's report—did Blake.

Bill:

TEAR THIS SHEET OUT WHEN YOU'VE READ IT!

Well, the worst has happened. We couldn't have asked fate to give us an unkindlier kick in the pants. I hate to think of Pelham being dead. What a man he was, what a friend! But we all knew the risk we were taking, he more than any of us. So all we can say is, "Sleep well, good friend. We'll never forget you."

But Renfrew's case is now serious. After all, we were worried, wondering how he'd take his first awakening, let alone a bang between the eyes like Pelham's death. And I think that the first anxiety was justified.

As you and I have always known, Renfrew was one of Earth's fair-haired boys. Just imagine any one human being born with his combination of looks, money and intelligence. His great fault was that he never let the future trouble him. With that dazzling personality of his, and the crew of worshipping women and yes-men around him, he didn't have much time for anything but the present.

Realities always struck him like a thunderbolt. He could

leave those three ex-wives of his—and they weren't so ex, if you ask me—without grasping that it was for ever.

That good-bye party was enough to put anyone into a sort of mental haze when it came to realities. To wake up a hundred years later, and realize that those he loved had withered, died and been eaten by worms—well-l-l!

(I deliberately put it as badly as that, because the human mind thinks of awfully strange angles, no matter how it censures speech.)

I personally counted on Pelham acting as a sort of psychological support to Renfrew; and we both knew that Pelham recognized the extent of his influence over Renfrew. That influence must be replaced. Try to think of something, Bill, while you're charging around doing routine work. We've got to live with that guy after we all wake up at the end of five hundred years.

Tear out this sheet. What follows is routine.   NED.

I burned the letter in the incinerator, examined the two sleeping bodies—how deathly quiet they lay—and then returned to the control room.

In the plate, the sun was a very bright star, a jewel set in black velvet, a gorgeous shining brilliant.

Alpha Centauri was brighter. It was a radiant light in that panoply of black and glitter. It was still impossible to make out the separate suns of Alpha A, B, C, and Proxima, but their combined light brought a sense of awe and majesty.

Excitement blazed inside me: and consciousness came of the glory of this trip we were making, the first men to head for far Centaurus, the first men to dare aspire to the stars.

Even the thought of Earth failed to dim that surging tide of wonder, the thought that seven, possibly eight generations, had been born since our departure; the thought that the girl who had given me the sweet remembrance of her red lips, was now known to her descendants as their great-great-great grandmother—if she were remembered at all.

The immense time involved, the whole idea, was too meaningless for emotion.

I did my work, took my third dose of the drug, and went to bed. The sleep found me still without a plan about Renfrew.

When I woke up, alarm bells were ringing.

I lay still. There was nothing else to do. If I had moved, consciousness would have slid from me. Though it was mental torture to even think it, I realized that, no matter what the danger, the quickest way was to follow my routine to the second and in every detail.

Somehow I did it. The bells clanged and *brrred*, but I lay there until it was time to get up. The clamor was hideous, as I passed through the control room. But I *passed* through and sat for half an hour sipping my soup.

The conviction came to me that if that sound continued much longer, Blake and Renfrew would surely waken from their sleep.

At last, I felt free to cope with the emergency. Breathing hard, I eased myself into the control chair, cut off the mind-wrecking alarms, and switched on the plates.

A fire glowed at me from the rear-view plate. It was a colossal *white* fire, longer than it was wide, and filling nearly a quarter of the whole sky. The hideous thought came to me that we must be within a few million miles of some monstrous sun that had recently roared into this part of space.

Frantically, I manipulated the distance estimators—and then for a moment stared in blank disbelief at the answers that clicked metallically on to the product plate.

Seven miles! *Only* seven miles! Curious is the human mind. A moment before, when I had thought of it as an abnormally shaped sun, it hadn't resembled anything but an incandescent mass. Abruptly, now I saw that it had a solid outline, an unmistakable material shape.

Stunned, I leaped to my feet because—

It was a spaceship! An enormous, mile-long ship. Rather—I sank back into my seat, subdued by the catastrophe I was witnessing, and consciously adjusting my mind—the flaming hell of what had been a spaceship. Nothing that had been alive could possibly still be conscious in that horror of ravenous fire. The only possibility was that the crew had succeeded in launching lifeboats.

Like a madman, I searched the heavens for a light, a glint of metal that would show the presence of survivors.

There was nothing but the night and the stars and the hell of burning ship.

After a long time, I noticed that it was farther away, and seemed to be receding. Whatever drive forces had matched its velocity to ours must be yielding to the fury of the energies that were consuming the ship.

I began to take pictures, and I felt justified in turning on the oxygen reserves. As it withdrew into the distance, the miniature nova that had been a torpedo-shaped space liner began to change color, to lose its white intensity. It became a red fire silhouetted against darkness. My last glimpse showed it as a long, dull glow that looked like nothing else than a cherry-colored nebula seen edge on, like a blaze reflecting from the night beyond a far horizon.

I had already, in between observations, done everything else required of me; and now, I re-connected the alarm system and, very reluctantly, my mind seething with speculation, returned to bed.

As I lay waiting for my final dosage of the trip to take effect, I thought: the great star system of Alpha Centauri must have inhabited planets. If my calculations were correct, we were only one point six light-years from the main Alpha group of suns, slightly nearer than that to red Proxima.

Here was proof that the universe had at least one other supremely intelligent race. Wonders beyond our wildest expectation were in store for us. Thrill on thrill of anticipation raced through me.

It was only at the last instant, as sleep was already grasping at my brain, that the realization struck that I had completely forgotten about the problem of Renfrew.

I felt no alarm. Surely, even Renfrew would come alive in that great fashion of his when confronted by a complex alien civilization.

Our troubles were over.

Excitement must have bridged that final one hundred and fifty years of time. Because, when I wakened, I thought:

"We're here! It's over, the long night, the incredible journey. We'll all be waking, seeing each other, as well as the civilization out there. Seeing too, the great Centauri suns."

The strange thing, it struck me as I lay there exulting, was that the time seemed long. And yet . . . yet I had been awake only three times, and only once for the equivalent of a full day.

In the truest sense of meaning, I had seen Blake and Renfrew—and Pelham—no more than a day and a half ago. I had had only thirty-six hours of consciousness since a pair of soft lips had set themselves against mine, and clung in the sweetest kiss of my life.

Then why this feeling that millenniums had ticked by, second on slow second? Why this eerie, empty awareness of a journey through fathomless, unending night?

Was the human mind so easily fooled?

It seemed to me, finally, that the answer was that *I* had been alive for those five hundred years, all my cells and my organs had existed, and it was not even impossible that some part of my brain had been horrendously aware throughout the entire unthinkable period.

And there was, of course, the additional psychological fact that I knew now that five hundred years had gone by, and that—

I saw with a mental start, that my ten minutes were up. Cautiously, I turned on the massager.

The gentle, padded hands had been working on me for about fifteen minutes when my door opened; the light clicked on, and there stood Blake.

The too-sharp movement of turning my head to look at him made me dizzy. I closed my eyes, and heard him walk across the room towards me.

After a minute, I was able to look at him again without seeing blurs. I saw then that he was carrying a bowl of the soup. He stood staring down at me with a strangely grim expression on his face.

At last, his long, thin countenance relaxed into a wan grin.

"Lo, Bill," he said. "*Ssshh!*" he hissed immediately. "Now, don't try to speak. I'm going to start feeding you this soup while you're still lying down. The sooner you're up, the better I'll like it."

He was grim again, as he finished almost as if it were an afterthought: "I've been up for two weeks."

He sat down on the edge of the bed, and ladled out a spoonful of soup. There was silence, then, except for the rustling sound of the massager. Slowly, the strength flowed through my body; and with each passing second, I became more aware of the grimness of Blake.

"What about Renfrew?" I managed finally, hoarsely. "He awake?"

Blake hesitated, then nodded. His expression darkened with frown; he said simply:

"He's mad, Bill, stark, staring mad. I had to tie him up. I've got him now in his room. He's quieter now, but at the beginning he was a gibbering maniac."

"Are you crazy?" I whispered at last. "Renfrew was never so sensitive as that. Depressed and sick, yes; but the mere passage of time, abrupt awareness that all his friends are dead, couldn't make him insane."

Blake was shaking his head. "It isn't only that. Bill—"

He paused, then: "Bill, I want you to prepare your mind for the greatest shock it's ever had."

I stared up at him with an empty feeling inside me. "What do you mean?"

He went on grimacing: "I know you'll be able to take it. So don't get scared. You and I, Bill, are just a couple of lugs. We're along because we went to U with Renfrew and Pelham. Basically, it wouldn't matter to insensitives like us whether we landed in 1,000,000 B.C. or A.D. We'd just look around and say: 'Fancy seeing you here, mug!' or 'Who was that pterodactyl I saw you with last night? That wasn't no pterodactyl; that was Unthahorsten's bulbous-brained wife.'"

I whispered: "Get to the point. What's up?"

Blake rose to his feet. "Bill, after I'd read your reports about, and seen the photographs of, that burning ship, I got an idea. The Alpha suns were pretty close two weeks ago, only about six months away at our average speed of five hundred miles a second. I thought to myself: 'I'll see if I can tune in some of their radio stations.'

"Well," he smiled wryly, "I got hundreds in a few minutes. They came in all over the seven wave dials, with bell-like clarity."

He paused; he stared down at me, and his smile was a sickly thing. "Bill," he groaned, "We're the prize fools in creation. When I told Renfrew the truth, he folded up like ice melting into water."

Once more, he paused; the silence was too much for my straining nerves.

"For Heaven's sake, man—" I began, And stopped. And lay there, very still. Just like that the lightning of understanding flashed on me. My blood seemed to thunder through my veins. At last, weakly, I said: "You mean—"

Blake nodded. "Yeah," he said. "That's the way it is. And they've already spotted us with their spy rays and energy screens. A ship's coming out to meet us.

"I only hope," he finished gloomily, "They can do something for Jim."

I was sitting in the control chair an hour later when I saw the glint in the darkness. There was a flash of bright silver, that exploded into size. The next instant, an enormous spaceship had matched our velocity less than a mile away.

Blake and I looked at each other. "Did they say," I said shakily, "that that ship left its hangar ten minutes ago?"

Blake nodded. "They can make the trip from Earth to Centauri in three hours," he said.

I hadn't heard that before. Something happened inside my brain. "What!" I shouted, "Why, it's taken us five hun—"

I stopped; I sat there. "Three hours!" I whispered. "How *could* we have forgotten human progress?"

In the silence that fell then, we watched a dark hole open in the clifflike wall that faced us. Into this cavern, I directed our ship.

The rear-view plate showed that the cave entrance was closing. Ahead of us lights flashed on, and focused on a door. As I eased our craft to the metal floor, a face flickered on to our radio plate.

"Cassellahat!" Blake whispered in my ear. "The only chap who's talked direct to me so far."

It was a distinguished, scholarly looking head and face that peered at us. Cassellahat smiled, and said:

"You may leave your ship, and go through the door you see."

I had a sense of empty spaces around us, as we climbed gingerly out into the vast receptor chamber. Interplanetary spaceship hangars were like that, I reminded myself. Only this one had an alien quality that—

"Nerves!" I thought sharply.

But I could see that Blake felt it, too. A silent duo, we filed through the doorway into a hallway that opened into a very large, luxurious room.

It was such a room as a king or a movie actress on set might have walked into without blinking. It was all hung with gorgeous tapestries—that is, for a moment, I thought they were tapestries; then I saw they weren't. They were—I couldn't decide.

I had seen expensive furniture in some of the apartments Renfrew maintained. But these settees, chairs, and tables glittered at us, as if they were made of a matching design of differently colored fires. No, that was wrong; they didn't glitter at all. They—

Once more I couldn't decide.

I had no time for more detailed examinations. For a man, arrayed very much as we were, was rising from one of the chairs. I recognized Casellahat.

He came forward, smiling. Then he slowed, his nose wrinkling. A moment later, he hastily shook our hands, then swiftly retreated to a chair ten feet away, and sat down rather primly.

It was an astoundingly ungracious performance. But I was glad that he had drawn back that way. Because, as he shook my hand so briefly, I had caught a faint whiff of perfume from him. It was a vaguely unpleasant odor; and, besides—a man using perfume in quantities!

I shuddered. What kind of foppish nonsense had the human race gone in for?

He was motioning us to sit down. I did so, wondering: Was this our reception? The erstwhile radio operator began:

"About your friend, I must caution you. He is a schizoid type, and our psychologists will be able to effect a temporary recovery only for the moment. A permanent cure will require a longer period, and your fullest co-operation. Fall in readily with all Mr. Renfrew's plans, unless, of course, he takes a dangerous turn.

"But now"—he squirted us a smile—"permit me to welcome you to the four planets of Centauri. It is a great moment for me, personally. From early childhood, I have been trained for the sole purpose of being your mentor and guide; and naturally I am overjoyed that the time has come when my exhaustive studies of the middle period American language and customs can be put to the practical use for which they were intended."

He didn't look overjoyed. He was wrinkling his nose in that funny way I had already noticed, and there was a generally pained expression on his face. But it was his words that shocked me.

"What do you mean," I asked, "studies in American? Don't people speak the universal language any more?"

"Of course"—he smiled—"but the language has developed to a point where—I might as well be frank—you would have difficulty understanding such a simple word as 'yeh'."

"Yeh?" Blake echoed.

"Meaning 'yes'."

"Oh!"

We sat silent. Blake chewing his lower lip. It was Blake who finally said:

"What kind of places are the Centauri planets? You said something on the radio about the population centers having reverted to the city structure again.

"I shall be happy," said Cassellahat, "to show you as many of our great cities as you care to see. You are our guests, and several million credits have been placed to your separate accounts for you to use as you see fit."

"Gee!" said Blake.

"I must, however," Cassellahat went on, "give you a warning. It is important that you do not disillusion our peoples about yourselves. Therefore, you must never wander around the streets, or mingle with the crowds in any way. Always, your contact should be via newsreels, radio, or from the *inside* of a closed machine. If you have any plan to marry, you must now finally give up the idea."

"I don't get it!" Blake said wonderingly; and he spoke for us both.

Cassellahat finished firmly: "It is important that no one becomes aware that you have an offensive physical odor. It might damage your financial prospects considerably.

"And now"—he stood up—"for the time being, I shall leave you. I hope you don't mind if I wear a mask in the future in your presence. I wish you well, gentlemen and—"

He paused, glanced past us, said, "Ah, here is your friend."

I whirled, and I could see Blake twisting, staring—

"Hi there, fellows," Renfrew said cheerfully from the door, then wryly: "Have we ever been a bunch of suckers?"

I felt choked. I raced up to him, caught his hand, hugged him. Blake was trying to do the same.

When we finally released Renfrew, and looked around, Cassellahat was gone.

Which was just as well. I had been wanting to punch him in the nose for his final remarks.

"Well, here goes!" Renfrew said.

He looked at Blake and me, grinned, rubbed his hands together gleefully, and added:

"For a week I've been watching, thinking up questions to ask this cluck and—"

He faced Cassellahat. "What," he began, "Makes the speed of light constant?"

Cassellahat did not even blink. "Velocity equals the cube of the cube root of gd," he said, "d being the depth of the space time continuum, g the total toleration or gravity, as you would say, of all the matter in that continuum."

"How are planets formed?"

"A sun must balance itself in the space that it is in. It throws out matter as a sea vessel does anchors. That's a very rough description. I could give it to you in mathematical formula, but I'd have to write it down. After all, I'm not a scientist. These are merely facts that I've known from childhood, or so it seems."

"Just a minute," said Renfrew, puzzled. "A sun throws this matter out without any pressure other than its—desire—to balance itself?"

Cassellahat stared at him. "Of course not. The reason, the pressure involved, is very potent, I assure you. Without such a balance, the sun would fall out of this space. Only a few bachelor suns have learned how to maintain stability without planets."

"A few what?" echoed Renfrew.

I could see that he had been jarred into forgetting the questions he had been intending to ask one by swift one. Cassellahat's words cut across my thought; he said:

"A bachelor sun is a very old, cooled class M star. The hottest one known has a temperature of one hundred and ninety degrees F., the coldest forty-eight. Literally, a bachelor is a rogue, crotchety with age. Its main feature is that it permits no matter, no planets, not even gases in its vicinity."

Renfrew sat silent, frowning, thoughtful. I seized the opportunity to carry on a train of thought.

"This business," I said, "of knowing all this stuff without being a scientist, interests me. For instance, back home every kid understood the atomic-rocket principle practically from the day he was born. Boys of eight and ten rode around in specially made toys, took them apart and put them together again. They *thought* rocket-atomic, and any new development in the field was just pie for them to absorb.

"Now, here's what I'd like to know: what is the parallel here to that particular angle?"

"The adeledicnander force," said Cassellahat. "I've already tried to explain it to Mr. Renfrew, but his mind seems to baulk at some of the most simple aspects."

Renfrew roused himself, grimaced. "He's been trying to tell me that electrons think; and I won't swallow it."

Cassellahat shook his head. "Not think; they don't think. But they have a psychology."

"Electronic psychology!" I said.

"Simply adeledicnander," Cassellahat replied. "Any child—"

Renfrew groaned: "I know. Any child of six could tell me."

He turned to us. "That's why I lined up a lot of questions. I figured that if we got a good intermediate grounding, we might be able to slip into this adeledicnander stuff the way their kids do."

He faced Cassellahat. "Next question," he said. "What—"

Cassellahat had been looking at his watch. "I'm afraid, Mr. Renfrew," he interrupted, "that if you and I are going to be on the ferry to the Pelham planet, we'd better leave now. You can ask your questions on the way."

"What's all this?" I chimed in.

Renfrew explained: "He's taking me to the great engineering laboratories in the European mountains of Pelham. Want to come along?"

"Not me," I said.

Blake shrugged. "I don't fancy getting into one of those suits Cassellahat has provided for us, designed to keep our odor in, but not theirs out."

He finished: "Bill and I will stay here and play poker for some of that five million credit's worth of dough we've got in the State bank."

Cassellahat turned at the door; there was a distinct frown

on the flesh mask he wore. "You treat our government gift very lightly."

"Yeih!" said Blake.

"So we stink," said Blake.

It was nine days since Cassellahat had taken Renfrew to the planet Pelham; and our only contact had been a radio telephone call from Renfrew on the third day, telling us not to worry.

Blake was standing at the window of our penthouse apartment in the city of Newmerica; and I was on my back on a couch, in my mind a mixture of thoughts involving Renfrew's potential insanity and all the things I had heard and seen about the history of the past five hundred years.

I roused myself. "Quit it," I said. "We're faced with a change in the metabolism of the human body, probably due to the many different foods from remote stars that they eat. They must be able to smell better, too, because just being near us is agony to Cassellahat, whereas we only notice an unpleasantness from him. It's a case of three of us against billions of them. Frankly, I don't see an early victory over the problem, so let's just take it quietly."

There was no answer; so I returned to my reverie. My first radio message to Earth had been picked up; and so, when the interstellar drive was invented in A.D. 2320, less than one hundred and forty years after our departure, it was realized what would eventually happen.

In our honor, the four habitable planets of the Alpha A and B suns were called Renfrew, Pelham, Blake, and Endicott. Since 2320, the populations of the four planets had become so dense that a total of nineteen billion people now dwelt on their narrowing land spaces. This in spite of migrations to the planets of more distant stars.

The space liner I had seen burning in A.D. 2511 was the only ship ever lost on the Earth-Centauri lane. Travelling at full speed, its screens must have reacted against our spaceship. All the automatics would instantly have flashed on; and, as those defences were not able at that time to stop a ship that had gone Minus Infinity, every recoil engine aboard had probably blown up.

Such a thing could not happen again. So enormous had been the progress in the adeledicnander field of power that the greatest liners could stop dead in the full fury of mid-flight.

We had been told not to feel any sense of blame for that one disaster, as many of the most important advances in adeledicnander electronic psychology had been made as the result of theoretical analyses of that great catastrophe.

I grew aware that Blake had flung himself disgustedly into a nearby chair.

"Boy, oh, boy," he said, "this is going to be some life for us. We can all anticipate about fifty more years of being pari-ahs in a civilization where we can't even understand how the simplest machines work."

I stirred uneasily. I had had similar thoughts. But I said nothing. Blake went on:

"I must admit, after I first discovered the Centauri planets had been colonized, I had pictures of myself bowling over some dame, and marrying her."

Involuntarily my mind leaped to the memory of a pair of lips lifting up to mine. I shook myself. I said:

"I wonder how Renfrew is taking all this. He—"

A familiar voice from the door cut off my words. "Renfrew," it said, "is taking things beautifully now that the first shock has yielded to resignation, and resignation to purpose."

We had turned to face him by the time he finished. Renfrew walked slowly towards us, grinning. Watching him, I felt uncertain as to just how to take his built-up sanity.

He was at his best. His dark, wavy hair was perfectly combed. His startlingly blue eyes made his whole face come alive. He was a natural physical wonder; and at his normal he had all the shine and swagger of an actor in a carefully tailored picture.

He wore that shine and swagger now. He said:

"I've bought a spaceship fellows. Took all my money and part of yours, too. But I knew you'd back me up. Am I right?"

"Why sure," Blake and I echoed.

Blake went on alone: "What's the idea?"

"I get it," I chimed in. "We'll cruise all over the universe, live our life span exploring new worlds. Jim, you've got something there. Blake and I were just going to enter a suicide pact."

Renfrew was smiling. "We'll cruise for a while anyway."

Two days later, Cassellahat having offered no objection and no advice about Renfrew, we were in space.

It was a curious three months that followed. For a while I felt a sense of awe at the vastness of the cosmos. Silent planets swung into our viewing plates, and faded into remoteness behind us, leaving nostalgic memory of uninhabited, windlashed forests and plains, deserted, swollen seas, and nameless suns.

The sight and the remembrance brought loneliness like an ache, and the knowledge, the slow knowledge, that this journeying was not lifting the weight of strangeness that had settled upon us ever since our arrival at Alpha Centauri.

There was nothing here for our souls to feed on, nothing that would satisfactorily fill one year of our life, let alone fifty.

I watched the realization grow on Blake, and I waited for a sign from Renfrew that he felt it, too. The sign didn't come. That of itself worried me; then I grew aware of something else. Renfrew was watching us. Watching us with a hint in his manner of secret knowledge, a suggestion of secret purpose.

My alarm grew; and Renfrew's perpetual cheerfulness didn't help any. I was lying on my bunk at the end of the third month, thinking uneasily about the whole unsatisfactory situation, when my door opened and Renfrew came in.

He carried a paralyser gun and a rope. He pointed the gun at me, and said:

"Sorry, Bill. Cassellahat told me to take no chances, so just lie quiet while I tie you up."

"Blake!" I bellowed.

Renfrew shook his head gently. "No use," he said. "I was in his room first."

The gun was steady in his fingers, his blue eyes were steely. All I could do was tense my muscles against the ropes as he tied me, and trust to the fact that I was twice as strong, at least, as he was.

I thought in dismay: Surely I could prevent him from tying me too tightly.

He stepped back finally, said again: "Sorry, Bill." He added: "I hate to tell you this, but both of you went off the deep end mentally when we arrived at Centauri; and this is the cure prescribed by the psychologists whom Cassellahat consulted. You're supposed to get a shock as big as the one that knocked you for a loop."

The first time I'd paid no attention to his mention of Cassellahat's name. Now my mind flared with understanding.

Incredibly, Renfrew had been told that Blake and I were mad. All these months he had been held steady by a sense of responsibility towards us. It was a beautiful psychological scheme. The only thing was: *what* shock was going to be administered?

Renfrew's voice cut off my thought. He said:

"It won't be long now. We're already entering the field of the bachelor sun."

"Bachelor sun!" I yelled.

He made no reply. The instant the door closed behind him, I began to work on my bonds; all the time I was thinking:

What was it Cassellahat had said? Bachelor suns maintained themselves in this space by a precarious balancing.

In *this* space! The sweat poured down my face, as I pictured ourselves being precipitated into another plane of the spacetime continuum—I could feel the ship falling when I finally worked my hands free of the rope.

I hadn't been tied long enough for the cords to interfere with my circulation. I headed for Blake's room. In two minutes we were on our way to the control cabin.

Renfrew didn't see us till we had him. Blake grabbed his gun; I hauled him out of the control chair with one mighty heave and dumped him onto the floor.

He lay there, unresisting, grinning up at us. "Too late," he taunted. "We're approaching the first point of intolerance, and there's nothing you can do except prepare for the shock."

I scarcely heard him. I plumped myself into the chair, and glared into the viewing plates. Nothing showed. That stumped me for a second. Then I saw the recorder instruments. They were trembling furiously, registering a body of INFINITE SIZE.

For a long moment I stared crazily at those incredible figures. Then I plunged the decelerator far over. Before that pressure of full-driven adeledicnander, the machine grew rigid; I had a sudden fantastic picture of two irresistible forces in full collision. Gasping, I jerked the power out of gear.

We were still falling.

"An orbit," Blake was saying. "Get us into an orbit."

With shaking fingers, I pounded one out on the keyboard, basing my figures on a sun of Sol-ish size, gravity, and mass.

The bachelor wouldn't let us have it.

I tried another orbit, and a third, and more—finally one that would have given us an orbit around mighty Antares itself. But the deadly reality remained. The ship plunged on, down and down.

And there was nothing visible on the plates, not a real shadow of substance. It seemed to me once that I could make out a vague blur of greater darkness against the black reaches of space. But the stars were few in every direction and it was impossible to be sure.

Finally, in despair, I whirled out of the seat, and knelt beside Renfrew, who was still making no effort to get up.

"Listen, Jim," I pleaded, "what did you do this for? What's going to happen?"

He was smiling easily. "Think," he said, "of an old, crusty, human bachelor. He maintains a relationship with his fellows, but the association is as remote as that which exists between a bachelor sun and the stars in the galaxy of which it is a part."

He added: "Any second now we'll strike the first period of intolerance. It works in jumps like quantum, each period being four hundred and ninety-eight years, seven months and eight days plus a few hours."

It sounded like gibberish. "But what's going to happen?" I urged. "For Heaven's sake, man!"

He gazed up at me blandly; and, looking at him, I had the sudden, wondering realization that he was sane, the old completely rational Jim Renfrew, made better somehow, stronger. He said quietly:

"Why, it'll just knock us out of its toleration area; and in doing so will put us back—"

JERK!

The lurch was immensely violent. With a bang, I struck the floor, skidded, and then a hand—Renfrew's—caught me. And it was all over.

I stood up, conscious that we were no longer falling. I looked at the instrument board. All the lights were dim, untroubled, the needles firmly at zero. I turned and stared at Renfrew, and at Blake, who was ruefully picking himself from the floor.

Renfrew said persuasively: "Let me at the control board, Bill. I want to set our course for earth."

For a long minute, I gazed at him; and then, slowly, I stepped aside. I stood by as he set the controls and pulled the accelerator over. Renfrew looked up.

"We'll reach Earth in about eight hours," he said, "and it'll be about a year and a half after we left five hundred years ago.

Something began to tug at the roof of my cranium. It took several seconds before I decided that it was probably my brain jumping with the tremendous understanding that suddenly flowed in upon me.

The bachelor sun, I thought dazedly. In easing us out of its field of toleration, it had simply precipitated us into a period of time beyond its field. Renfrew had said . . . had said that it worked in jumps of . . . four hundred and ninety-eight years and some seven months and—

But what about the ship? Wouldn't the twenty-seventh century adeledicnander brought to the twenty-second century, before it was invented, change the course of history? I mumbled the question.

Renfrew shook his head. "Do *we* understand it? Do we even dare monkey with the raw power inside those engines? I'll say not. As for the ship, we'll keep it for our own private use."

"B-but—" I began.

He cut me off. "Look, Bill," he said, "here's the situation: that girl who kissed you—don't think I didn't see you falling like a ton of bricks—is going to be sitting beside you fifty years from now, when *your* voice from space reports to Earth that you had wakened on your first lap of the first trip to Centauris."

That's exactly what happened.

the monster

THE great ship poised a quarter of a mile above one of the cities. Below was a cosmic desolation. As he floated down in his energy bubble, Enash saw that the buildings were crumbling with age.

"No sign of war damage!" The bodiless voice touched his ears momentarily. Enash tuned it out.

On the ground he collapsed his bubble. He found himself in a walled enclosure overgrown with weeds. Several skeletons lay in the tall grass beside the rakish building. They were of long, two-legged, two-armed beings with the skulls in each case mounted at the end of a thin spine. The skeletons, all of adults, seemed in excellent preservation, but he bent down and touched one, a whole section of it crumbled into a fine powder. As he straightened, he saw that Yoal was floating down nearby. Enash waited until the historian had stepped out of his bubble, then he said:

"Do you think we ought to use our method of reviving the long dead?"

Yoal was thoughtful. "I have been asking questions of the various people who have landed, and there is something wrong here. This planet has no surviving life, not even insect life. We'll have to find out what happened before we risk any colonization."

Enash said nothing. A soft wind was blowing. It rustled through a clump of trees nearby. He motioned toward the trees. Yoal nodded and said, "Yes, the plant life has not been harmed, but plants after all are not affected in the same way as the active life forms."

There was an interruption. A voice spoke from Yoal's receiver: "A museum has been found at approximately the center of the city. A red light has been fixed on the roof."

Enash said, "I'll go with you, Yoal. There might be skeletons of animals and of the intelligent being in various

30

stages of his evolution. You didn't answer my questions. Are you going to revive these beings?"

Yoal said slowly, "I intend to discuss the matter with the ccuncil, but I think there is no doubt. We must know the cause of this disaster." He waved one sucker vaguely to take in half the compass. He added as an afterthought, "We shall proceed cautiously, of course, beginning with an obviously early development. The absence of the skeletons of children indicates that the race had developed personal immortality."

The council came to look at the exhibits. It was, Enash knew, a formal preliminary only. The decision was made. There would be revivals. It was more than that. They were curious. Space was vast, the journeys through it long and lonely, landing always a stimulating experience, with its prospect of new life forms to be seen and studied.

The museum looked ordinary. High-domed ceilings, vast rooms. Plastic models of strange beasts, many artifacts—too many to see and comprehend in so short a time. The life span of a race was imprisoned here in a progressive array of relics. Enash looked with the other, and was glad when they came to the line of skeletons and preserved bodies. He seated himself behind the energy screen, and watched the biological experts take a preserved body out of a stone sarcophagus. It was wrapped in windings of cloth, many of them. The experts did not bother to unravel the rotted material. Their forceps reached through, pinched a piece of skull—that was the accepted procedure. Any part of the skeleton could be used, but the most perfect revivals, the most complete reconstruction resulted when a certain section of the skull was used.

Hamar, the chief biologist, explained the choice of the body. "The chemicals used to preserve this mummy show a sketchy knowledge of chemistry. The carvings on the sarcophagus indicate a crude and unmechanical culture. In such a civilization there would not be much development of the potentialities of the nervous system. Our speech experts have been analysing the recorded voice mechanism which is a part of each exhibit, and though many languages are involved—evidence that the ancient language spoken at the time the body was alive has been reproduced—they found no difficulty in translating the meanings. They have now adapted our universal speech machine, so that anyone who wishes to need only speak into his communicator, and so will have his words

translated into the language of the revived person. The reverse, naturally, is also true. Ah, I see we are ready for the
first body."

Enash watched intently with the others as the lid was
clamped down on the plastic reconstructor, and the growth
processes were started. He could feel himself becoming tense.
For there was nothing haphazard about what was happening.
In a few minutes a full-grown ancient inhabitant of this
planet would sit up and stare at them. The science involved
was simple and always fully effective.

. . . Out of the shadows of smallness, life grows. The level
of beginning and ending, of life and—not life; in that dim
region matter oscillates easily between old and new habits.
The habit of organic, or the habit of inorganic. Electrons do
not have life and un-life values. Atoms know nothing of in-
animateness. But when atoms form into molecules, there is a
step in the process, one tiny step, that is of life—if life begins
at all. One step, and then darkness. Or aliveness.

A stone or a living cell. A grain of gold or a blade of
grass, the sands of the sea or the equally numerous animal-
cules inhabiting the endless fishy waters—the difference is
there in the twilight zone of matter. Each living cell has in it
the whole form. The crab grows a new leg when the old one
is torn from its flesh. Both ends of the planarian worm elon-
gate, and soon there are two worms, two identities, two
digestive systems each as greedy as the original, each a whole,
unwounded, unharmed by its experience. Each cell can be the
whole. Each cell remembers in a detail so intricate that no to-
tality of words could ever describe the completeness achieved.

But—paradox—memory is not organic. An ordinary wax
record remembers sounds. A wire recorded easily gives up a
duplicate of the voice that spoke into it years before.
Memory is a physiological impression, a mark on matter, a
change in the shape of a molecule, so that when a reaction is
desired the *shape* emits the same rhythm of response.

Out of the mummy's skull had come the multi-quadrillion
memory shapes from which a response was now being
evoked. As ever, the memory held true.

A man blinked, and opened his eyes.

"It is true, then," he said aloud, and the words were translated into the Ganae tongue as he spoke them. "Death is

merely an opening into another life—but where are my attendants?" At the end, his voice took on a complaining tone.

He sat up, and climbed out of the case, which had automatically opened as he came to life. He saw his captors. He froze, but only for a moment. He had a pride and a very special arrogant courage, which served him now. Reluctantly, he sank to his knees and made obeisance, but doubts must have been strong in him. "Am I in the presence of the gods of Egyptus?" He climbed to his feet. "What nonsense is this? I do not bow to nameless demons."

Captain Gorsid said, "Kill him?"

The two-legged monster dissolved, writhing, in the beam of a ray gun.

The second revived man stood up, pale, and trembled with fear. "My God I swear I won't touch the stuff again. Talk about pink elephants—"

Yoal was curious. "To what *stuff* do you refer, revived one?"

"The old hooch, the poison in the hip-pocket flask, the juice they gave me at that speak . . . my lordie!"

Captain Gorsid looked questioningly at Yoal, "Need we linger?" Yoal hesitated. "I am curious." He addressed the man. "If I were to tell you that we were visitors from another star, what would be your reaction?"

The man stared at him. He was obviously puzzled, but the fear was stronger. "Now, look," he said, "I was driving along, minding my own business. I admit I'd had a shot or two too many, but it's the liquor they serve these days. I swear I didn't see the other car—and if this is some new idea of punishing people who drink and drive, well, you've won. I won't touch another drop as long as I live, so help me."

Yoal said, "He drives a "car" and thinks nothing of it. Yet we saw no cars. They didn't even bother to preserve them in the museums."

Enash noticed that everyone waited for everyone else to comment. He stirred as he realized the circle of silence would be complete unless he spoke. He said, "Ask him to describe the car. How does it work?"

"Now, you're talking," said the man. "Bring on your line of chalk, and I'll walk it, and ask any questions you please. I may be so tight that I can't see straight, but I can always drive. How does it work? You just put her in gear and step on the gas."

"Gas," said engineering officer Veed. "The internal combustion engine. That places him."

Captain Gorsid motioned to the guard with the ray gun.

The third man sat up, and looked at them thoughtfully. "From the stars?" he said finally. "Have you a system, or was it blind chance?"

The Ganae councillors in that domed room stirred uneasily in their curved chairs. Enash caught Yoal's eye on him. The shock in the historian's eyes alarmed the meteorologist. He thought: "The two-legged one's adjustment to a new situation, his grasp of realities, was abnormally rapid. No Ganae could have equalled the swiftness of the reaction."

Hamar, the chief biologist, said, "Speed of thought is not necessarily a sign of superiority. The slow, careful thinker has his place in the hierarchy of intellect."

But Enash found himself thinking, it was not the speed, it was the accuracy of the response. He tried to imagine himself being revived from the dead, and understanding instantly the meaning of the presence of aliens from the stars. He couldn't have done it.

He forgot his thought, for the man was out of the case. As Enash watched with the others, he walked briskly over to the window and looked out. One glance, and then he turned back.

"Is it all like this?" he asked.

Once again, the speed of his understanding caused a sensation. It was Yoal who finally replied.

"Yes. Desolation. Death. Ruin. Have you any idea as to what happened?"

The man came back and stood in front of the energy screen that guarded the Ganae. "May I look over the museum? I have to estimate what age I am in. We had certain possibilities of destruction when I was last alive, but which one was realized depends on the time elapsed."

The councillors looked at Captain Gorsid, who hesitated; then, "Watch him," he said to the guard with the ray gun. He faced the man. "We understand your aspirations fully. You would like to seize control of this situation and ensure your own safety. Let me reassure you. Make no false moves, and all will be well."

Whether or not the man believed the lie, he gave no sign. Nor did he show by a glance or a movement that he had seen the scarred floor where the ray gun had burned his two predecessors into nothingness. He walked curiously to the nearest doorway, studied the other guard who waited there for him, and then, gingerly, stepped through. The first guard followed him, then came the mobile energy screen, and finally, trailing one another, the councillors.

Enash was the third to pass through the doorway. The room contained skeletons and plasic models of animals. The room beyond that was what, for want of a better term, Enash called a culture room. It contained the artifacts from a single period of civilization. It looked very advanced. He had examined some of the machines when they first passed through it, and had thought: Atomic energy. He was not alone in his recognition. From behind him, Captain Gorsid said to the man:

"You are forbidden to touch anything. A false move will be the signal for the guards to fire."

The man stood at ease in the center of the room. In spite of a curious anxiety, Enash had to admire his calmness. He must have known what his fate would be, but he stood there thoughtfully, and said finally, deliberately, "I do not need to go any farther. Perhaps you will be able to judge better than I of the time that has elapsed since I was born and these machines were built. I see over there an instrument which, according to the sign above it, counts atoms when they explode. As soon as the proper number have exploded it shuts off the power automatically, and for just the right length of time to prevent a chain explosion. In my time we had a thousand crude devices for limiting the size of an atomic reaction, but it required two thousand years to develop those devices from the early beginnings of atomic energy. Can you make a comparison?"

The councillors glanced at Veed. The engineering officer hesitated. At last, reluctantly, he said, "Nine thousand years ago we had a thousand methods of limiting atomic explosions." He paused, then even more slowly, " I have never heard of an instrument that counts out atoms for such a purpose."

"And yet," murmured Shuri, the astronomer, breathlessly, "the race was destroyed."

There was silence. It ended as Gorsid said to the nearest guard, "Kill the monster!"

But it was the guard who went down, bursting into flame. Not just one guard, but the guards! Simultaneously down, burning with blue flame. The flame licked at the screen, recoiled, and licked more furiously, recoiled and burned brighter. Through a haze of fire, Enash saw that the man had retreated to the far door, and that the machine that counted atoms was glowing with a blue intensity.

Captain Gorsid shouted into his communicator, "Guard all exits with ray guns. Spaceships stand by to kill alien with heavy guns."

Somebody said, "Mental control. Some kind of mental control. What have we run into?"

They were retreating. The blue flame was at the ceiling, struggling to break through the screen. Enash had a last glimpse of the machine. It must still be counting atoms, for it was a hellish blue. Enash raced with the others to the room where the man had been resurrected. There, another energy screen crashed to their rescue. Safe now, they retreated into their separate bubbles and whisked through outer doors and up to the ship. As the great ship soared, an atomic bomb hurtled down from it. The mushroom of flame blotted out the museum and the city below.

"But we still don't know why the race died," Yoal whispered into Enash's ear, after the thunder had died from the heavens behind them.

The pale yellow sun crept over the horizon on the third morning after the bomb was dropped, the eighth day since the landing. Enash floated with the others down on a new city. He had come to argue against any further revival.

"As a meteorologist," he said, "I pronounce this planet safe for Ganae colonization. I cannot see the need for taking any risks. This race has discovered the secrets of its nervous system, and we cannot afford—"

He was interrupted. Hamar the biologist, said dryly, "If they knew so much why didn't they migrate to other star systems and save themselves?"

"I will concede," said Enash, "that very possibly they had not discovered our system of locating stars with planetary families." He looked earnestly around the circle of his friends. "We have agreed that was a unique accidental discovery. We were lucky, not clever."

He saw by the expressions on their faces that they were mentally refuting his arguments. He felt a helpless sense of imminent catastrophe. For he could see that picture of a great race facing death. It must have come swiftly, but not so swiftly that they didn't know about it. There were too many skeletons in the open, lying in the gardens of magnificent homes, as if each man and his wife had come out to wait for the doom of his kind. He tried to picture it for the council, that last day long, long ago, when a race had calmly met its ending. But his visualization failed somehow, for the others shifted impatiently in the seats that had been set up behind the series of energy screens, and Captain Gorsid said, "Exactly what aroused this intense emotional reaction in you, Enash?"

The question gave Enash pause. He hadn't thought of it as emotional. He hadn't realized the nature of his obsession, so subtly had it stolen upon him. Abruptly now, he realized.

"It was the third one," he said, slowly. "I saw him through the haze of energy fire, and he was standing there in the distant doorway watching us curiously, just before we turned to run. His bravery, his calm, the skilful way he had duped us—it all added up."

"Added up to his death!" said Yamar. And everybody laughed.

"Come now, Enash," said Vice-Captain Mayad good-humoredly, "you're not going to pretend that this race is braver than our own, or that, with all the precautions we have now taken, we need fear one man?"

Enash was silent, feeling foolish. The discovery that he had had an emotional obsession abashed him. He did not want to appear unreasonable. He made a final protest, "I merely wish to point out," he said doggedly, "that this desire to discover what happened to a dead race does not seem absolutely essential to me."

Captain Gorsid waved at the biologist, "Proceed," he said, "with the revival."

To Enash, he said, "Do we dare return to Gana, and recommend mass migrations—and then admit that we did not actually complete our investigations here? It's impossible, my friend."

It was the old argument, but reluctantly now Enash admitted there was something to be said for that point of view. He forgot that, for the fourth man was stirring.

The man sat up. And vanished.

There was a blank, startled horrified silence. Then Captain Gorsid said harshly, "He can't get out of there. We know that. He's in there somewhere."

All around Enash, the Ganae were out of their chairs, peering into the energy shell. The guards stood with ray guns held limply in their suckers. Out of the corner of his eye, he saw one of the protective screen technicians beckon to Veed, who went over. He came back grim. He said, "I'm told the needles jumped ten points when he first disappeared. That's on the neucleonic level."

"By ancient Ganae!" Shuri whispered. "We've run into what we've always feared."

Gorsid was shouting into the communicator. "Destroy all the locators on the ship. Destroy them, do you hear!"

He turned with glaring eyes. "Shuri," he bellowed, "they don't seem to understand, Tell those subordinates of yours to act. All locators and reconstructors must be destroyed."

"Hurry, hurry!" said Shuri weakly.

When that was done they breathed more easily. There were grim smiles and tensed satisfaction, "At least," said Vice-Captain Mayad, "he cannot now ever discover Gana. Our great system of locating suns with planets remains our secret. There can be no retaliation for—" he stopped, said slowly, "What am I talking about? We haven't done anything. We're not responsible for the disaster that has befallen the inhabitants of his planet."

But Enash knew what he had meant. The guilt feelings came to the surface at such moments as this—the ghosts of all the races destroyed by the Ganae, the remorseless will that had been in them, when they first landed, to annihilate whatever was here. The dark abyss of voiceless hate and terror that lay behind them; the days on end when they had mercilessly poured poisonous radiation down upon the unsuspecting inhabitants of peaceful planets—all that had been in Mayad's words.

"I still refuse to believe he has escaped." That was Captain Gorsid. "He's in there. He's waiting for us to take down our screens, so he can escape. Well, we won't do it."

There was silence again as they stared expectantly into the emptiness of the energy shell. The reconstructor rested on its metal supports, a glittering affair. But there was nothing else. Not a flicker of unnatural light or shade. The yellow rays of the sun bathed the open spaces with a brilliance that left no room for concealment.

"Guards," said Gorsid, "destroy the reconstructor. I thought he might come back to examine it, but we can't take a chance on that."

It burned with a white fury. And Enash, who had hoped somehow that the deadly energy would force the two-legged thing into the open, felt his hopes sag within him.

"But where can he have gone?" Yoal whispered.

Enash turned to discuss the matter. In the act of swinging around, he saw that the monster was standing under a tree a score of feet to one side, watching them. He must have arrived at *that* moment, for there was a collective gasp from the councillors. Everybody drew back. One of the screen technicians, using great presence of mind jerked up an energy screen between the Ganae and the monster. The creature came forward slowly. He was slim of build, he held his head well back. His eyes shone as from an inner fire.

He stopped as he came to the screen, reached out and touched it with his fingers. It flared, blurred with changing colors. The colors grew brighter, and extended in an intricate pattern all the way from his head to the ground. The blur cleared. The pattern faded into invisibility. The man was through the screen.

He laughed, a soft curious sound; then sobered. "When I first awakened," he said, "I was curious about the situation. The question was, What should I do with you?"

The words had a fateful ring to Enash on the still morning air of that planet of the dead. A voice broke the silence, a voice so strained and unnatural that a moment passed before he recognized it as belonging to Captain Gorsid.

"*Kill him*"

When the blasters ceased their effort, the unkillable thing remained standing. He walked slowly forward until he was only a half dozen feet from the nearest Ganae. Enash had a position well to the rear. The man said slowly:

"Two courses suggest themselves, one based on gratitude for reviving me, the other based on reality. I know you for what you are. Yes, *know* you—and that is unfortunate. It is hard to feel merciful. To begin with," he went on, "let us suppose you surrender the secret of the locator. Naturally, now that a system exists, we shall never be caught as we were."

Enash had been intent, his mind so alive with the potentialities of the disaster that was here that it seemed impossible that he could think of anything else. And yet, a part of his attention was stirred now. "What did happen?" he asked.

The man changed color. The emotions of that far day thickened his voice. "A nucleonic storm. It swept in from outer space. It brushed this edge of our galaxy. It was about ninety-light-years in diameter, beyond the farthest limit of our power. There was no escape from it. We had dispensed with spaceships, and had no time to construct any. Castor, the only star with planets ever discovered by us, was also in the path of the storm." He stopped. "The secret?" he said.

Around Enash, the councillors were breathing easier. The fear of race destruction that had come to them was lifting. Enash saw with pride that the first shock was over, and they were not even afraid for themselves.

"Ah," said Yoal softly, "you don't know the secret. In spite of all your great developments, we alone can conquer the galaxy." He looked at the others, smiling confidently. "Gentlemen," he said, "our pride in a great Ganae achievement is justified. I suggest we return to our ship. We have no further business on this planet."

There was a confused moment while their bubbles formed, when Enash wondered if the two-legged one would try to stop their departure. But when he looked back, he saw that the man was walking in leisurely fashion along a street.

That was the memory Enash carried with him, as the ship began to move. That and the fact that the three atomic bombs they dropped, one after the other, failed to explode.

"We will not," said Captain Gorsid, "give up a planet as easily as that. I propose another interview with the creature."

They were floating down again into the city, Enash and Yoal and Veed and the commander. Captain Gorsid's voice tuned in once more:

"... As I visualize it"—through the mist Enash could see the transparent glint of the other three bubbles around him—"we jumped to conclusions about this creature, not justified by the evidence. For instance, when he awakened, he vanished. Why? Because he was afraid, of course. He wanted to size up the situation. *He* didn't believe he was omnipotent."

It was sound logic. Enash found himself taking heart from it. Suddenly he was astonished that he had become panicky so easily. He began to see the danger in a new light. Only one man alive on a new planet. If they were determined enough, colonists could be moved in as if he did not exist. It had been done before, he recalled. On several planets, small groups of the original populations had survived the destroying radiation, and taken refuge in remote areas. In almost every case, the new colonists gradually hunted them down. In two instances, however, that Enash remembered, native races were still holding small sections of their planets. In each case, it had been found impractical to destroy them because it would have endangered the Ganae on the planet. So survivors were tolerated. One man would not take up very much room.

When they found him, he was busy sweeping out the lower floor of a small bungalow. He put the broom aside and stepped on to the terrace outside. He had put on sandals, and he wore a loose-fitting robe made of very shiny material. He eyed them indolently but he said nothing.

It was Captain Gorsid who made the proposition. Enash had to admire the story he told into the language machine. The commander was very frank. That approach had been decided on. He pointed out that the Ganae could not be expected to revive the dead of this planet. Such altruism would be unnatural considering that the ever-growing Ganae hordes had a continual need for new worlds. Each vast new population increment was a problem that could be solved by one method only. In this instance, the colonists would gladly respect the rights of the sole survivor of this world.

It was at this point that the man interrupted. "But what is the purpose of this endless expansion?" he seemed genuinely curious. "What will happen when you finally occupy every planet in this galaxy?"

Captain Gorsid's puzzled eyes met Yoal's, then flashed to Veed, then Enash. Enash shrugged his torso negatively, and felt pity for the creature. The man didn't understand, possibly never could understand. It was the old story of two different viewpoints, the virile and the decadent, the race that aspired to the stars and the race that declined the call of destiny.

"Why not," urged the man, "control the breeding chambers?"

"And have the government overthrown!" said Yoal.

He spoke tolerantly, and Enash saw that the others were smiling at the man's *naïveté*. He felt the intellectual gulf between them widening. The creature had no comprehension of the natural life forces that were at work. The man spoke again:

"Well, if you don't control them, we will control them for you."

There was silence.

They began to stiffen. Enash felt it in himself, saw the signs of it in the others. His gaze flicked from face to face, then back to the creature in the doorway. Not for the first time, Enash had the thought that their enemy seemed helpless, "Why," he decided, "I could put my suckers around him and crush him."

He wondered if mental control of nucleonic, nuclear, and gravitonic energies included the ability to defend oneself from a macrocosmic attack. He had an idea it did. The exhibition of power two hours before might have had limitations, but if so, it was not apparent. Strength or weakness could make no difference. The threat of threats had been made "If you don't control—we will."

The words echoed in Enash's brain, and, as the meaning penetrated deeper, his aloofness faded. He had always regarded himself as a spectator. Even when, earlier, he had argued against the revival, he had been aware of a detached part of himself watching the scene rather than being a part of it. He saw with a sharp clarity that that was why he had finally yielded to the conviction of the others. Going back beyond that to remoter days, he saw that he had never quite considered himself a participant in the seizure of the planets of other races. He was the one who looked on, and thought of reality, and speculated on a life that seemed to have no meaning. It was meaningless no longer. He was caught by a tide of irresistible emotion, and swept along. He felt himself sinking, merging with the Ganae mass being. All the strength and all the will of the race surged up in his veins.

He snarled, "Creature, if you have any hopes of reviving your dead race, abandon them now."

The man looked at him, but said nothing. Enash rushed on, "If you could destroy us, you would have done so already. But the truth is that you operate within limitations. Our ship is so built that no conceivable chain reaction could be started in it. For every plate of potential unstable materials in it there is a counteracting plate, which prevents the development of a critical pile. You might be able to set off explosions in our engines, but they, too, would be limited, and would merely start the process for which they are intended—confined in their proper space."

He was aware of Yoal touching his arm. "Careful," warned the historian. "Do not in your just anger give away vital information."

Enash shook off the restraining sucker. "Let us not be unrealistic," he said harshly. "This thing has divined most of our racial secrets, apparently merely by looking at our bodies. We would be acting childishly if we assumed that he has not already realized the possibilities of the situation."

"*Enash!*" Captain Gorsid's voice was imperative.

As swiftly as it had come, Enash's rage subsided. He stepped back. "Yes, commander."

"I think I know what you intended to say," said Captain Gorsid. "I assure you I am in full accord, but I believe also that I, as top Ganae official, should deliver the ultimatum."

He turned. His horny body towered above the man. "You have made the unforgivable threat. You have told us, in effect, that you will attempt to restrict the vaulting Ganae spirit."

"Not the spirit," said the man. He laughed softly. "No, not the spirit."

The commander ignored the interruption. "Accordingly, we have no alternative. We are assuming that, given time to locate the materials and develop the tools, you might be able to build a reconstructor. In our opinion it will be at least two years before you can complete it, *even if you know how*. It is an immensely intricate machine, not easily assembled by the lone survivor of a race that gave up its machines millennia before disaster struck.

"You did not have time to build a spaceship. We won't give you time to build a reconstructor.

"Within a few minutes our ship will start dropping bombs. It is possible you will be able to prevent explosions in your vicinity. We will start, accordingly, on the other side of the planet. If you stop us there, then we will assume we need help. In six months of travelling at top acceleration, we can reach a point where the nearest Ganae planet would hear our messages. They will send a fleet so vast that all your powers of resistance will be overcome. By dropping a hundred or a thousand bombs every minute, we will suceed in devastating every city so that not a grain of dust will remain of the skeletons of your people.

"That is our plan. So it shall be. Now, do your worst to us who are at your mercy."

The man shook his head. "I shall do nothing—now!" he said. He paused, then thoughtfully, "Your reasoning is fairly accurate. Fairly. Naturally, I am not all powerful, but it seems to me you have forgotten one little point. I won't tell you what it is. And now," he said, "good day to you. Get back to your ship, and be on your way. I have much to do."

Enash had been standing quietly, aware of the fury building up in him again. Now, with a hiss, he sprang forward, suckers outstretched. They were almost touching the smooth flesh—when something snatched at him.

He was back on the ship.

He had no memory of movement, no sense of being dazed or harmed. He was aware of Veed and Yoal and Captain Gorsid standing near him as astonished as he himself. Enash remained very still, thinking of what the man had said: ". . . *Forgotten one little point.*" Forgotten? That meant they knew. What could it be? He was still pondering about it when Yoal said:

"We can be reasonably certain our bombs alone will not work."

They didn't.

Forty light-years out from Earth, Enash was summoned to the council chambers. Yoal greeted him wanly, "the monster is aboard."

The thunder of that poured through Enash, and with it came a sudden comprehension. "That was what he meant we had forgotten," he said finally, aloud and wonderingly. "That he can travel through space at will within a limit—what was the figure he once used?—of ninety light-years."

He sighed. He was not surprised that the Ganae, who had to use ships, would not have thought immediately of such a possibility. Slowly, he began to retreat from the reality. Now that the shock had come, he felt old and weary, a sense of his mind withdrawing again to its earlier state of aloofness. It required a few minutes to get the story. A physicist's assistant, on his way to the storeroom, had caught a slimpse of a man in a lower corridor. In such a heavily manned ship, the wonder was that the intruder had escaped earlier observation. Enash had a thought.

"But after all we are not going all the way to one of our planets. How does he expect to make use of us to locate it if we only use the video—" He stopped. That was it, of course. Directional video beams would have to be used, and the man would travel in the right direction the instant contact was made.

Enash saw the decision in the eyes of his companions, the only possible decision under the circumstances. And yet, it seemed to him they were missing some vital point. He walked slowly to the great video plate at one end of the chamber. There was a picture on it, so sharp, so vivid, so majestic that the unaccustomed mind would have reeled as from a stunning blow. Even to him, who knew the scene, there came a constriction, a sense of unthinkable vastness. It was a video view of a section of the milky way. Four hundred *million* stars as seen through telescopes that could pick up the light of a red dwarf at thirty thousand light-years.

The video plate was twenty-five yards in diameter—a scene that had no parallel elsewhere in the plenum. Other galaxies simply did not have that many stars.

Only one in two hundred thousand of those glowing suns had planets.

That was the colossal fact that compelled them now to an irrevocable act. Wearily, Enash looked around him.

"The monster has been very clever," he said quietly. "If we go ahead, he goes with us, obtains a reconstructor, and returns by his method to his planet. If we use the directional beam, he flashes along it, obtains a reconstructor, and again reaches his planet first. In either event, by the time our fleet arrived back here, he would have revived enough of his kind to thwart any attack we could mount."

He shook his torso. The picture was accurate, he felt sure, but it still seemed incomplete. He said slowly, "We have one advantage now. Whatever decision we make, there is no language machine to enable him to learn what it is. We can carry out our plans without his knowing what they will be. He knows that neither he nor we can blow up the ship. That leaves us one real alternative."

It was Captain Gorsid who broke the silence that followed. "Well, gentlemen, I see we know our minds. We will set the engines, blow up the controls, and take him with us."

They looked at each other, race pride in their eyes. Enash touched suckers with each in turn.

An hour later, when the heat was already considerable, Enash had the thought that sent him staggering to the communicator, to call Shuri, the astronomer. "Shuri," he yelled, "when the monster first awakened—remember Captain Gorsid had difficulty getting your subordinates to destroy the locators. We never thought to ask them what the delay was. Ask them . . . ask them—"

There was a pause, then Shuri's voice came weakly over the roar of the static, "They . . . couldn't . . . get . . . into the . . . room. The door was locked."

Enash sagged to the floor. They had missed more than one point, he realized. The man had awakened, realized the situation; and, when he vanished, he had gone to the ship, and there discovered the secret of the locator and possibly the secret of the reconstructor—if he didn't know it previously. By the time he reappeared, he already had from them what he wanted. All the rest must have been designed to lead them to this act of desperation.

In a few moments, now, *he* would be leaving the ship, secure in the knowledge that shortly no alien mind would know his planet existed. Knowing, too, that his race would live again, and this time never die.

Enash staggered to his feet, clawed at the roaring communicator, and shouted his new understanding into it. There was no answer. It clattered with the static of uncontrollable and inconceivable energy. The heat was peeling his armoured hide as he struggled to the matter transmitter. It flashed at him with purple flame. Back to the communicator he ran shouting and screaming.

He was still whimpering into it a few minutes later when the mighty ship plunged into the heart of a blue-white sun.

dormant

OLD was the island. Even the thing that lay in the outer channel, exposed to the rude wash of the open sea, had never guessed, when it was alive a million million years before, that here was a protuberance of primeval earth itself.

The island was roughly three miles long and, at its widest, half a mile across. It curved tensely around a blue lagoon and the thin shape of its rocky, foam-ridden arms and hands came down toward the toe of the island—like a gigantic man bending over, striving to touch his feet and not quite making it.

Through the channel made by that gap between the toes and the fingers came the sea.

The water resented the channel. With an endless patience it fought to break the wall of rock, and the tumult of the waters was a special sound, a blend of all that was raucous and unseemly in the eternal quarrel between resisting land and encroaching wave.

At the very hub of the screaming waters lay Iilah, dead now almost for ever, forgotten by time and the universe.

Early in 1941, Japanese ships came and ran the gauntlet of dangerous waters into the quiet lagoon. From the deck of one of the ships a pair of curious eyes pondered the thing, where it lay in the path of the rushing sea. But the owner of those eyes was the servant of a goverment that frowned on extramilitary ventures on the part of its personnel. And so the engineer Taku Onilo merely noted in his report that, "At the mouth of this channel there lies a solid shape of glittery, rocklike substance about four hundred feet long and ninety feet wide."

The little yellow men built their underground gas and oil tanks and departed toward the setting sun. The water rose and fell, rose and fell again. The days and the years drifted by, and the hand of time was heavy. The seasonal rains arrived on their rough schedule and washed away the marks of man. Green growth sprouted where machines had exposed the raw earth. The war ended. The underground tanks sagged a little in their beds of earth and cracks appeared in several main pipes. Slowly the oil drained off and for years a yellow-green oil slick brightened the gleam of the lagoon waters.

In the reaches of Bikini Atoll, hundreds of miles away, first one explosion, then another, started in motion an intricate pattern of radio-activated waters. The first seepage of that potent energy reached the island in the early autumn of 1946.

It was about two years later that a patient clerk ransacking the records of the Imperial Japanese Navy in Tokyo, reported the existence of the oil tanks. In due time—1950—the destroyer *Coulson* set forth on its routine voyage of examination.

The time of the nightmare was come.

Lieutenant Keith Maynard peered gloomily through his binoculars at the island. He was prepared to find something wrong, but he expected a distracting monotony of sameness, not something radically different. "Usual undergrowth," he muttered, "and a backbone of semi-mountain running like a framework the length of the island trees—" He stopped there.

A broad swath had been cut through the palms on the rear shoreline. They were not just down. They were crushed deep into a furrow that was already alive with grass and small growth. The furrow, which looked about a hundred feet wide, led upward from the beach to the side of a hill, to where a large rock lay half buried near the top of the hill.

Puzzled, Maynard glanced down at the Japanese photographs of the island. Involuntarily, he turned towards his executive officer, Lieutenant Gerson. "Good lord!" he said. "How did that rock get up *there*? It's not on any photographs."

The moment he had spoken he regretted it. Gerson looked at him, with his usual faint antagonism, shrugged and said, "Maybe we've got the wrong island."

Maynard did not answer that. He considered Gerson a queer character. The man's tongue dripped ceaselessly with irony.

"I'd say it weighs about two million tons. The Japs probably dragged it up there to confuse us."

Maynard said nothing. He was annoyed that he had made

a comment. Particularly annoyed because, for a moment, he had actually thought of the Japs in connection with the rock. The weight estimate, which he instantly recognized as probably fairly accurate, ended all his wilder thoughts. If the Japs could move a rock weighing two million tons they had also won the war. Still, it was very curious and deserved investigation—later.

They ran the channel without incident. It was wider and deeper than Maynard had understood from the Jap accounts, which made everything easy. Their midday meal was eaten in the shelter of the lagoon. Maynard noted the oil on the water and issued immediate warnings against throwing matches overboard. After a brief talk with the other officers, he decided that they would set fire to the oil as soon as they had accomplished their mission and were out of the lagoon.

About one-thirty, boats were lowered and they made shore in quick order. In an hour, with the aid of transcribed Japanese blueprints, they located the four buried tanks. It took somewhat longer to assess the dimensions of the tanks and to discover that three of them were empty. Only the smallest, containing high-octane petrol, remained leakproof and still full. The value of that was about seventeen thousand dollars, not worth the attention of the large navy tankers that were still cruising around, picking up odd lots of Japanese and American material. Maynard presumed that a lighter would eventually be dispatched for the petrol, but that was none of his business.

In spite of the speed with which his job had been accomplished, Maynard climbed wearily up to the deck just as darkness was falling. He must have overdone it a little because Gerson said too loudly, "Worn out, sir?"

Maynard stiffened. And it was that comment, rather than any inclination, that decided him not to postpone his exploration of the rock. As soon as possible after the evening meal, he called for volunteers. It was pitch dark as the boat, with seven men and Bos'n's Mate Yewell and himself, was beached on the sands under the towering palms. The party headed inland.

There was no moon and the stars were scattered among remnant clouds of the rainy season just past. They walked in the furrow where the trees had been literally ploughed into the ground. In the pale light of the flashlights the spectacle of numerous trees, burned and planed into a smoothed levelness with the soil, was unnatural.

Maynard heard one of the men rumble, "Must have been some freak of a typhoon did that."

Not only a typhoon, Maynard decided but a ravenous fire followed by a monstrous wind, so monstrous that—his thought paused. He couldn't imagine any storm big enough to lift a two-million-ton rock to the side of a hill a quarter of a mile long and four hundred feet above sea level. From nearby, the rock looked like nothing more than rough granite. In the beam of the flashlights it glinted with innumerable streaks of pink. Maynard led his party alongside it and the vastness of it grew upon him as he climbed past its four hundred feet of length and peered up at gleaming walls, like cliffs looming above him. The upper end, buried though it was deeper into the ground, rose at least fifty feet above his head.

The night had grown uncomfortably warm. Maynard was perspiring freely. He enjoyed a moment of weary pleasure in the thought that he was doing his duty under unpleasant circumstances. He stood uncertain, gloomily savoring the intense primitive silence of the night. "Break off some samples here and there" he said finally. "Those pink streaks look interesting."

It was a few seconds later that a man's scream of agony broke through the thrall of darkness.

Flashlights blinked on. They showed Seaman Hicks twisting on the ground beside the rock. In the bright flame of the lights the man's wrist showed as a smouldering, blackened husk with the entire hand completely burned off.

He had touched Iilah.

Maynard gave the desperately suffering man morphine and they rushed him back to the ship. Radio contact was established with base and a consulting surgeon gave cut by cut instructions on the operation. It was agreed that a hospital plane would be despatched for the patient. There must have been some puzzlement at headquarters as to how the accident had occurred, because "further information" was requested about the "hot" rock. By morning the people at the other end were calling it a meteorite. Maynard, who did not normally question opinions offered by his superiors, frowned over the identification, and pointed out that this meteorite weighed two million tons and rested on the surface of the island.

"I'll send the assistant engineer officer to take its temperature," he said.

An engine-room thermometer registered the rock's surface temperature at eight hundred-odd degrees Fahrenheit. The answer to that was a question that shocked Maynard.

"Why, yes," he replied, "we're getting mild radio-active reactions from the water, but nothing else. And nothing serious. Under the circumstances we'll withdraw from the lagoon at once and await the ships with the scientists."

He ended the conversation, pale and shaken. Nine men, including himself, had walked along within a few yards of the rock, well within the deadly danger zone. In fact, even the *Coulson*, more than half a mile away, would have been affected.

But the gold leaves of the electroscope stood out stiff and the Geiger-Mueller counter clucked only when placed in the water and then only at long intervals. Relieved, Maynard went down to have another look at Seaman Hicks. The injured man slept uneasily but he was not dead, which was a good sign. When the hospital plane arrived there was a doctor aboard, who attended Hicks and then gave everyone on the destroyer a blood-count test. He came up on deck, a cheerful young man, and reported to Maynard.

"Well, it can't be what they suspect," he said. "Everybody's O.K. even Hicks, except for his hand. That burned awfully quick, if you ask me, for a temperature of only eight hundred."

"I think his hand stuck," said Maynard. And he shuddered. In his self-destructive fashion, he had mentally experienced the entire accident.

"So that's the rock," said Dr. Clason. "Does seem odd how it got there."

They were still standing there five minutes later when a hideous screaming from below deck made a discordant sound on the still air of that remote island lagoon.

Something stirred in the depths of Iilah's awareness of himself, something that he had intended to do. He couldn't remember what.

That was the first real thought he had in late 1946, when

he felt the impact of outside energy. And stirred with returning life. The outside flow waxed and waned. It was abnormally, abysmally dim. The crust of the planet that he knew
had palpitated with the ebbing but potent energies of a world
not yet cooled from its sun state. It was only slowly that Iilah
realized the extent of the disaster that was his environment. At
first he was inwardly inclined, too pallidly alive to be interested in externals.

He forced himself to become more conscious of his environment. He looked forth with his radar vision out upon a
strange world. He was lying on a shallow plateau near the
top of a mountain. The scene was desolate beyond his
memory. There was not a glint nor pressure of atomic fire—
not a bubble of boiling rock nor a swirl of energy heaved
skyward by some vast interior explosion.

He did not think of what he saw as an island surrounded
by an apparently limitless ocean. He saw the land below the
water as well as above it. His vision based as it was on ultra-
ultra short waves, could not see water. He recognized that he
was on an old and dying planet, where life had long since become extinct. Alone and dying on a forgotten planet—if he
could only find the source of the energy that had revived
him.

By a process of simple logic he started down the mountain
in the direction from which the current of atomic energy
seemed to be coming. Somehow, he found himself below it
and had to levitate himself heavily back up. Once started upward, he headed for the nearest peak, with the intention of
seeing what was on the other side.

As he propelled himself out of the invisible, unsensed
waters of the lagoon, two diametrically opposed phenomena
affected him. He lost all contact with the water-borne current
of atomic energy. And, simultaneously, the water ceased to
inhibit the neutron and deuteron activity of his body. His life
took on an increased intensity. The tendency to slow stifle-
ment ended. His great form became a self-sustaining pile, capable of surviving for the normal radio-active lifespan of the
elements that composed it—still on an immensely less than
normal activity level for him. Again, Iilah thought, "There
was something I was going to do."

There was an increased flow of electrons through a score
of gigantic cells as he strained to remember. It slowed gradu-

ally when no memory came. The fractional increase of his life energy brought with it a wider, more exact understanding of his situation. Wave on wave of perceptive radaric forces flowed from him to the Moon, to Mars, to all the planets of the Solar System—and the echoes that came back were examined with an alarmed awareness that out there, too, were dead bodies.

He was caught in the confines of a dead system, prisoned until the relentless exhaustion of his material structure brought him once more to *rapport* with the barren mass of the planet on which he was marooned. He realized now that he had been dead. Just how it had happened he could not recall, except that explosively violent, frustrating substance had belched around him, buried him, and snuffed out his life processes. The atomic chemistry involved must eventually have converted the stuff into a harmless form, no longer capable of hindering him. But he was dead by then.

Now he was alive again, but in so dim a fashion that there was nothing to do but wait for the end. He waited.

In 1950 he watched the destroyer float towards him through the sky. Long before it slowed and stopped just below him, he had discovered that it was not a life-form related to him. It manufactured a dull internal heat and, through its exterior walls, he could see the vague glow of fires.

All that first day, Iilah waited for the creature to show awareness of him. But not a wave of life emanated from it. And yet it floated in the sky above the plateau, an impossible phenomenon, outside all his experience. To Iilah, who had no means of sensing water, who could not even imagine air, and whose ultra waves passed through human beings as if they did not exist, the reaction could mean only one thing—here was an alien life-form that had adapted itself to the dead world around him.

Gradually, Iilah grew excited. The thing could move freely above the surface of the planet. It would know if any source of atomic energy remained anywhere. The problem was to get into communication with it. The sun was high on the meridian of another day when Iilah directed the first questioning pattern of thought towards the destroyer. He aimed straight at the vaguely glowing fires in the engine room, where, he reasoned, would be the intelligence of the alien creature.

The thirty-four men who died in the spaces in and around the engine room and the fire room were buried on the shore. Their surviving comrades expected to stay there until the abandoned *Coulson* ceased to give off dangerous radio-active energies. On the seventh day, when transport planes were already dumping scientific equipment and personnel, three of the men fell sick and their blood count showed a fateful decrease in the number of red corpuscles. Although no orders had arrived, Maynard took alarm and ordered the entire crew shipped for observation to Hawaii.

He allowed the officers to make their own choice, but advised the second engineer officer, the first gunnery officer and several ensigns who had helped hoist the dead men up to the deck, to take no chances, but to grab space on the first planes. Although all were ordered to leave, several crew members asked permission to remain. And, after a careful questioning by Gerson, a dozen men who could prove that they had not been near the affected area, were finally allowed to stay.

Maynard would have preferred to see Gerson himself depart, but in this he was disappointed. Of the officers who had been aboard the destroyer at the time of the disaster, Lieutenants Gerson, Lausson, and Haury, the latter two being gunnery officers, and Ensigns McPelty, Roberts, and Manchioff, remained on the beach.

Among the higher ratings remaining behind were the chief commissary steward, Jenkins, and chief bos'n's mate, Yewell.

The navy group was ignored except that several times requests were made that they move their tents out of the way. Finally, when it seemed evident that they would be crowded out once more, Maynard, in annoyance, ordered the canvas moved well down the coast, where the palms opened up to form a grassy meadow.

Maynard grew puzzled, then grim, as the weeks passed and no orders arrived concerning the disposal of his command. In one of the Stateside papers that began to follow the scientists, the bulldozers, and cement mixers on to the island he read an item in an "inside" column that gave him his first inkling. According to the columnists, there had been a squabble between navy bigwigs and the civilian members of the Atomic Energy Commission over control of the investigation. With the result that the navy had been ordered to "stay out".

Maynard read the account with mixed feelings and a dawning understanding that he was *the* navy representative on the island. The realization included a thrilling mental visualization of himself rising to the rank of admiral—if he handled the situation right. Just what would be right, aside from keeping a sharp eye on everything, he couldn't decide. It was an especially exquisite form of self-torture.

He couldn't sleep. He spent his days wandering as unobtrusively as possible through the ever vaster encampment of the army of scientists and their assistants. At night he had several hiding places from which he watched the brilliantly lighted beach.

It was a fabulous oasis of brightness in the dark vaulting vastness of a Pacific night. For a full mile, string upon string of lights spread along the whispering waters. They silhouetted and spotlighted the long, thick, back-curving, cement-like walls that reared up eerily, starting at the rim of the hill. Protective walls that were already soaring up around the rock itself, striving to block it off from all outside contact. Always, at midnight, the bulldozers ceased their roarings, the cement-mixing trucks dumped their last loads and scurried down the makeshift beach road to silence. The already intricate organization settled into an uneasy slumber. Maynard usually waited with the painful patience of a man doing more than his duty. About one o'clock, he too would make his way to bed.

The secret habit paid off. He was the only man who actually witnessed the rock climb to the top of the hill.

It was a stupendous event. The time was about a quarter to one and Maynard was on the point of calling it a day when he heard the sound. It was like a truck emptying a load of gravel. For a bare moment he thought of it entirely in relation to his hiding place. His night-spying activities were going to be found out. An instant after that the rock reared up into the brilliance of the lights.

There was a roaring now of cement barriers crumbling before that irresistible movement. Fifty, sixty, then ninety feet of monster rock loomed up above the hill, slid with a heavy power over the crown, and stopped.

For two months Iilah had watched the freighters breast the channel. Just why they followed that route interested him. And he wondered if there was some limitation on them that kept them at such an exact level. What was more interesting by far, however, was that in every case the aliens would slide around the island, and disappear behind a high promontory that was the beginning of the east shore. In every case, after they had been gone for a few days, they would slide into view again, glide through the channel, and gradually move off through the sky.

During these months, Iilah caught tantalizing glimpses of small, but much faster, winged ships that shot down from a great height and disappeared behind the crest of the hill to the east. Always to the east. His curiosity grew enormous, but he was reluctant to waste energy. He grew aware finally of a nighttime haze of lights that brightened the eastern sky at night. He set off the more violent explosions on his lower surface which made directive motion possible, and climbed the last seventy or so feet to the top of the hill. He regretted it immediately.

One ship lay a short distance offshore. The haze of lights along the eastern slope seemed to have no source. As he watched, scores of trucks and bulldozers raced around, some of them coming quite close to him. Just what they wanted, or what they were doing he could not make out. He sent several questioning thought-waves at various of the objects, but there was no response.

He gave it up as a bad job.

The rock was still resting on the top of the hill the next morning, poised so that both sides of the island were threatened by the stray bursts of energy which it gave off so erratically. Maynard heard his first account of the damage done from Jenkins, the chief commissary steward. Seven truck drivers and two bulldozer men dead, a dozen men suffering from glancing burns—and two months' labor wrecked.

There must have been a conference among the scientists, for shortly after noon, trucks and bulldozers, loaded with equipment, began to stream past the navy camp. A seaman, dispatched to follow them, reported that they were setting up camp on the point at the lower end of the island.

Just before dark a notable event took place. The director of the Project together with four executive scientists walked into the lighted area and asked for Maynard. The group was smiling and friendly. There was handshaking all around. Maynard introduced Gerson who, unfortunately, as far as

Maynard was concerned, was in camp at the moment. And then the visiting delegation got down to business.

"As you know," said the director, "the *Coulson* is only partially radio-active. The rear gun turret is quite unaffected, and we accordingly request that you co-operate with us and fire on the rock until it is broken into sections."

It took Maynard a moment to recover from his astonishment, and to know what he would answer to that. At no time, during the next few days, did he question the belief of the scientists that the rock should be broken up and so rendered harmless. He refused their request and then doggedly continued to refuse it. It was not until the third day that he thought of a reason.

"Your precautions, gentlemen," he said, "are not sufficient. I do not consider that moving the camp out to the point is safeguard enough in the event that the rock should blow up. Now, of course, if I should receive a command from a naval authority to do as you wish . . ."

He left that sentence dangling, and saw from their disappointed faces that there must have been a feverish exchange of radio messages with their own headquarters. The arrival of a Kwajalein paper on the fourth day quoted a "high" Washington naval officer as saying that, "any such decisions must be left to the judgment of the naval commander on the island." It was also stated that, if a properly channelled request was made, the navy would be glad to send an atomic expert of its own to the scene.

It was obvious to Maynard that he was handling the situation exactly as his superiors desired. The only thing was that, even as he finished reading the account, the silence was broken by the unmistakable bark of a destroyer's five-inch guns, that sharpest of all gunfire sounds.

Unsteadily Maynard climbed to his feet. He headed for the nearest height. Before he reached it the second shattering roar came from the other side of the lagoon, and once again an ear-splitting explosion echoed from the vicinity of the rock. Maynard reached his vantage point and, through his binoculars, saw about a dozen men scurrying over the aft deck in and about the rear gun turret. A new and grimmer fury came against the camp director. He was determined that every man assisting on the destroyer must be arrested for malicious and dangerous trespass.

He did think vaguely that it was a sorry day indeed when inter-bureau squabbles could cause such open defiance of the armed forces, as if nothing more was involved than struggle for power. But that thought faded as swiftly as it came.

He waited for the third firing, then hurried down the hill to his camp. Swift commands to the men and officers sent eight of them to positions along the shore of the island, where they could watch boats trying to land. With the rest, Maynard headed towards the nearest navy boat. He had to take the long way around, by way of the point, and there must have been radio communication between the point and those on the ship, for a motor-boat was just appearing around the far end of the island when Maynard approached the now silent and deserted *Coulson*.

He hesitated. Should he give chase? A careful study of the rock proved it to be apparently unbroken. The failure cheered him, but also made him cautious. It wouldn't do for his superiors to discover that he had not taken the necessary precautions to prevent the destroyer being boarded.

He was still pondering the problem when Iilah started down the hill, straight towards the destroyer.

Iilah saw the first bright puff from the destroyers' guns. And then he had a moment during which he observed an object flash towards him. In the old, old times he had developed defences against hurtling objects. Quite automatically now, he tensed for the blow of this one. The object, instead of merely striking him with its hardness, exploded. The impact was stupendous. His protective crust cracked. The concussion blurred and distorted the flow from every electronic plate in his great mass.

Instantly, the automatic stabilizing "tubes" sent out balancing impulses. The hot, internal, partly rigid, partly fluid matter that made up the greater portion of his body, grew hotter, more fluidic. The weaknesses induced by that tremdous concussion accepted the natural union of a liquid, hardening quicker under enormous pressures. Sane again, Iilah considered what had happened. An attempt at communication?

The possibility excited him. Instead of closing the gap in his outer wall he hardened the matter immediately behind it, thus cutting off wasteful radiation. He waited. Again the hurtling object, and the enormously potent blow, as it struck him . . .

After a dozen blows, each with its resulting disaster to his protective shell, Iilah writhed with doubts. If these were messages he could not receive them, or understand. He began reluctantly to allow the chemical reactions that sealed the protective barrier. Faster than he could seal the holes, the hurtling objects breached his defences.

And still he did not think of what had happened as an attack. In all his previous existence he had never been attacked in such a fashion. Just what methods had been used against him Iilah could not remember. But certainly nothing so purely molecular.

The conviction that it was an attack came reluctantly, and he felt no anger. The reflex of defence in him was logical, not emotional. He studied the destroyer and it seemed to him that his purpose must be to drive it away. It would also be necessary to drive away every similar creature that tried to come near him. All the scurrying objects he had seen when he counted the crest of the hill—all that must depart.

He started down the hill.

The creature floating above the plateau had ceased exuding flame. As Iilah eased himself near it, the only sign of life was a smaller object that darted alongside it.

There was a moment then when Iilah entered the water. That was a shock. He had almost forgotten that there was a level of this desolate mountain below which his life forces were affected.

He hesitated. Then slowly, he slid further down into the depressing area, conscious that he had attained a level of strength that he could maintain against such a purely negative pressure.

The destroyer began to fire at him. The shells delivered at point-blank range, poked deep holes into the ninety-foot cliff with which Iilah faced his enemy. As that wall of rock touched the destroyer, the firing stopped. (Maynard and his men, having defended the *Coulson* as long as possible, tumbled over the far side into their boat and raced away as fast as possible.).

Iilah shoved. The pain that he felt from those titanic blows was the pain that comes to all living creatures experiencing partial dissolution. Laboriously, his body repaired itself. And with anger and hatred and fear now, he shoved. In a few minutes he had tangled the curiously unwieldy structure in the rocks that rose up to form the edge of the plateau. Beyond was the sharp declining slope of the mountain.

An unexpected thing happened. Once among the rocks, the creature started to shudder and shake, as if caught by some inner destructive force. It fell over on its side and lay there like some wounded thing, quivering and breaking up.

It was an amazing spectacle. Iilah withdrew from the water, reclimbed the mountain, and plunged down into the sea on the other side, where a freighter was just getting under way. It swung around the promontory, and successfully floated through the channel and out, coasting along high above the bleak valley that fell away beyond the breakers. It moved along for several miles, then slowed and stopped.

Iilah would have liked to chase it further, but he was limited to ground movement. And so, the moment the freighter had stopped, he turned and headed towards the point, where the small objects were cluttered. He did not notice the men who plunged into the shallows near the shore and, from that comparative safety, watched the destruction of their equipment. Iilah left a wake of burning and crushed vehicles. The few drivers who tried to get their machines away became splotches of flesh and blood inside and on the metal of their machines.

There was a fantastic amount of stupidity and panic. Iilah moved at a speed of about eight miles an hour. Three hundred and seventeen men were caught in scores of individual traps and crushed by a monster that did not even know they existed. Each man must have felt himself personally pursued.

Afterward, Iilah climbed to the nearest peak and studied the sky for further interlopers. Only the freighter remained, a shadowy threat some four miles away.

Darkness cloaked the island slowly. Maynard moved cautiously through the grass, flashing his flashlight directly in front of him on a sharp downward slant. Every little while he called out, "Anybody around?" It had been like that for hours now. Through the fading day they had searched for survivors, each time loading them aboard their boat and ferrying them through the channel and out to where the freighter waited.

The orders had come through by radio. They had forty-eight hours to get clear of the island. After that the bomb run would be made by a drone plane.

Maynard pictured himself walking along on this monster-inhabited, night-enveloped island. And the shuddery thrill that came was almost pure unadulterated pleasure. He felt himself pale with a joyous terror. It was like the time his ship had been among those shelling a Jap-held beach. He had been gloomy until, suddenly, he had visualized himself out there on the beach at the receiving end of the shells. He began to torture himself with the possibility that, somehow, he might be left behind when the freighter finally withdrew.

A moan from the near darkness ended that thought. In the glow of the flashlight Maynard saw a vaguely familiar face. The man had been smashed by a falling tree. As executive officer Gerson came forward and administered morphine, Maynard bent closer to the injured man and peered at him anxiously. It was one of the world-famous scientists on the island. Ever since the disaster the radio messages had been asking for him. There was not a scientific body on the globe that cared to commit itself to the navy bombing plan until he had given his opinion.

"Sir," began Maynard, "what do you think about—" He stopped. He settled mentally back on his heels.

Just for a moment he had forgotten that the naval authorities had already ordered the atomic bomb dropped, after being given goverment authority to do as they saw fit.

The scientist stirred. "Maynard," he croaked, "there's something funny about that creature. Don't let them do any—" His eyes grew bright with pain. His voice trailed.

It was time to push questions. The great man would soon be deep in a doped sleep and he would be kept that way. In a moment it would be too late.

The moment passed.

Lieutenant Gerson climbed to his feet. "There, that ought to do it, captain." He turned to the seaman carrying the stretchers. "Two of you take this man back to the boat. Careful. I've put him to sleep."

Maynard followed the stretcher without a word. He had a sense of having been saved from the necessity of making a decision, rather than of having made one.

The night dragged on.

Morning dawned grayly. Shortly after the sun came up, a tropical shower stormed across the island and rushed off eastward. The sky grew amazingly blue and the world of water all around seemed motionless, so calm did the sea become.

Out of the blue distance, casting a swiftly moving shadow on that still ocean, flew the drone plane. Long before it came in sight, Iilah sensed the load it carried. He quivered through his mass. Enormous electron tubes waxed and waned with expectancy and, for a brief while, he thought it was one of his own kind coming near.

As the plane drew closer he sent cautious thoughts toward it. Several planes, to which he had directed his thought waves, had twisted jerkily in mid-air and tumbled down out of control. But this one did not deviate from its course. When it was almost directly overhead a large object dropped from it, turned lazily over and over as it curved towards Iilah. It was set to explode about a hundred feet above the target.

The timing was perfect, the explosion titanic.

As soon as the blurring effects of so much new energy had passed, the now fully alive Iilah thought in a quiet, rather startled comprehension, "Why, of course, that's what I was trying to remember. That's what I was supposed to do."

He was puzzled that he could have forgotten. He had been sent during the course of an interstellar war—which apparently was still going on. He had been dropped on the planet under enormous difficulties and had been instantly snuffed out by enemy frustrators. Now, he was ready to do his job.

He took test sightings on the sun and on the planets that were within reach of his radar signals. Then he set in motion a process that would dissolve all the shields inside his own body. He gathered his pressure forces for the final thrust that would bring the vital elements hard together at exactly the calculated moment.

The explosion that knocked a planet out of its orbit was recorded on every seismograph on the globe. It would be some time, however, before astronomers would discover that earth was falling into the sun. And no man would live to see Sol flare into nova brightness, and burn up the Solar System before gradually sinking back into a dim G state.

Even if Iilah had known that it was not the same war that had raged ten thousand million centuries before, he would have had no choice but to do as he did.

Robot atom bombs do not make up their own minds.

the enchanted village

"EXPLORERS of a new frontier" they had been called before they left for Mars.

For a while, after the ship crashed into a Martian desert, killing all on board except—miraculously—this one man, Bill Jenner spat the words occasionally into the constant, sand-laden wind. He despised himself for the pride he had felt when he first heard them.

His fury faded with each mile that he walked, and his black grief for his friends became a gray ache. Slowly he realized that he had made a ruinous misjudgement.

He had underestimated the speed at which the rocketship had been travelling. He'd guessed that he would have to walk three hundred miles to reach the shallow, polar sea he and the others had observed as they glided in from outer space. Actually, the ship must have flashed an immensely greater distance before it hurtled down out of control.

The days stretched behind him, seemingly as numberless as the hot, red, alien sand that scorched through his tattered clothes. A huge scarecrow of a man, he kept moving across the endless, arid waste—he would not give up.

By the time he came to the mountain, his food had long been gone. Of his four water bags, only one remained, and that was so close to being empty that he merely wet his cracked lips and swollen tongue whenever his thirst became unbearable.

Jenner climbed high before he realized that it was not just another dune that had barred his way. He paused, and as he gazed up at the mountain that towered above him, he cringed a little. For an instant he felt the hopelessness of this mad race he was making to nowhere—but he reached the top. He saw that below him was a depression surrounded by hills as high as, or higher than, the one on which he stood. Nestled in the valley they made was a village.

He could see trees and the marble floor of a courtyard. A score of buildings were clustered around what seemed to be a central square. They were mostly low-constructed, but there were four towers pointing gracefully into the sky. They shone in the sunlight with a marble luster.

Faintly, there came to Jenner's ears a thin, high-pitched whistling sound. It rose, fell, faded completely, then came up again clearly and unpleasantly. As Jenner ran toward it, the noise grated on his ears, eerie and unnatural.

He kept slipping on smooth rock, and bruised himself when he fell. He rolled halfway down into the valley. The buildings remained new and bright when seen from nearby. Their walls flashed with reflections. On every side was vegetation—reddish-green shubbery, yellow-green trees laden with purple and red fruit.

With ravenous intent, Jenner headed for the nearest fruit tree. Close up, the tree looked dry and brittle. The large red fruit he tore from the lowest branch, however, was plump and juicy.

As he lifted it to his mouth, he remembered that he had been warned during his training period to taste nothing on Mars until it had been chemically examined. But that was meaningless advice to a man whose only chemical equipment was in his own body.

Nevertheless, the possibility of danger made him cautious. He took his first bite gingerly. It was bitter to his tongue, and he spat it out hastily. Some of the juice which remained in his mouth seared his gums. He felt the fire of it, and he reeled from nausea. His muscles began to jerk, and he lay down on the marble to keep himself from falling. After what seemed like hours to Jenner, the awful trembling finally went out of his body and he could see again. He looked up despisingly at the tree.

The pain finally left him, and slowly he relaxed. A soft breeze rustled the dry leaves. Nearby trees took up that gentle clamor, and it struck Jenner that the wind here in the valley was only a whisper of what it had been on the flat desert beyond the mountain.

There was no other sound now. Jenner abruptly remembered the high-pitched, ever-changing whistle he had heard.

He lay very still, listening intently, but there was only the rustling of the leaves. The noisy shrilling had stopped. He wondered if it had been an alarm, to warn the villagers of his approach.

Anxiously he climbed to his feet and fumbled for his gun. A sense of disaster shocked through him. It wasn't there. His mind was a blank, and then he vaguely recalled that he had first missed the weapon more than a week before. He looked around him uneasily, but there was not a sign of creature life. He braced himself. He couldn't leave, as there was nowhere to go. If necessary, he would fight to the death to remain in the village.

Carefully Jenner took a sip from his water bag, moistening his cracked lips and his swollen tongue. Then he replaced the cap and started through a double line of trees toward the nearest building. He made a wide circle to observe it from several vantage points. On one side a low, broad archway opened into the interior. Through it, he could dimly make out the polished gleam of a marble floor.

Jenner explored the buildings from the outside, always keeping a respectful distance between him and any of the entrances. He saw no sign of animal life. He reached the far side of the marble platform on which the village was built, and turned back decisively. It was time to explore interiors.

He chose one of the four tower buildings. As he came within a dozen feet of it, he saw that he would have to stoop low to get inside.

Momentarily, the implications of that stopped him. These buildings had been constructed for a life form that must be very different from human beings.

He went forward again, bent down, and entered reluctantly, every muscle tensed.

He found himself in a room without furniture. However, there were several low marble fences projecting from one marble wall. They formed what looked like a group of four wide, low stalls. Each stall had an open trough carved out of the floor.

The second chamber was fitted with four inclined planes of marble, each of which slanted up to a dais. Altogether there were four rooms on the lower floor. From one of them a circular ramp mounted up, apparently to a tower room.

Jenner didn't investigate the upstairs. The earlier fear that he would find alien life was yielding to the deadly conviction that he wouldn't. No life meant no food or chance of getting any. In frantic haste he hurried from building to building, peering into the silent rooms, pausing now and then to shout hoarsely.

Finally there was no doubt. He was alone in a deserted village on a lifeless planet, without food, without water—except for the pitiful supply in his bag—and without hope.

He was in the fourth and smallest room of one of the tower buildings when he realized that he had come to the end of his search. The room had a single stall jutting out from one wall. Jenner lay down wearily in it. He must have fallen asleep instantly.

When he awoke he became aware of two things, one right after the other. The first realization occurred before he opened his eyes—the whistling sound was back; high and shrill, it wavered at the threshold of audibility.

The other was that a fine spray of liquid was being directed down at him from the ceiling. It had an odor, of which technician Jenner took a single whiff. Quickly he scrambled out of the room, coughing, tears in his eyes, his face already burning from chemical reaction.

He snatched his handkerchief and hastily wiped the exposed parts of his body and face.

He reached the outside and there paused, striving to understand what had happened.

The village seemed unchanged.

Leaves trembled in a gentle breeze. The sun was poised on a mountain peak. Jenner guessed from its position that it was morning again and that he had slept at least a dozen hours. The glaring white light suffused the valley. Half hidden by trees and shrubbery, the buildings flashed and shimmered.

He seemed to be in an oasis in a vast desert. It was an oasis, all right, Jenner reflected grimly, but not for a human being. For him, with its poisonous fruit, it was more like a tantalizing mirage.

He went back inside the building and cautiously peered into the room where he had slept. The spray of gas had stopped, not a bit of odor lingered, and the air was fresh and clean.

He edged over the threshold, half inclined to make a test. He had a picture in his mind of a long-dead Martian creature lazing on the floor in the stall while a soothing chemical sprayed down on its body. The fact that the chemical was deadly to human beings merely emphasized how alien to man was the life that had spawned on Mars. But there seemed little doubt of the reason for the gas. The creature was accustomed to taking a morning shower.

Inside the "bathroom," Jenner eased himself feet first into the stall. As his hips came level with the stall entrance, the solid ceiling sprayed a jet of yellowish gas straight down upon his legs. Hastily Jenner pulled himself clear of the stall. The gas stopped as suddenly as it had started.

He tried it again, to make sure it was merely an automatic process. It turned on, then shut off.

Jenner's thirst-puffed lips parted with excitement. He thought, "If there can be one automatic process, there may be others."

Breathing heavily, he raced into the outer room, Carefully he shoved his legs into one of the two stalls. The moment his hips were in, a streaming gruel filled the trough beside the wall.

He stared at the greasy-looking stuff with a horrified fascination—food—and drink. He remembered the poison fruit and felt repelled, but he forced himself to bend down and put his finger into the hot, wet substance. He brought it up, dripping, to his mouth.

It tasted flat and pulpy, like boiled wood fibre. It trickled viscously into his throat. His eyes began to water and his lips drew back convulsively. He realized he was going to be sick, and ran for the outer door—but didn't quite make it.

When he finally got outside, he felt limp and unutterably listless. In that depressed state of mind, he grew aware again of the shrill sound.

He felt amazed that he could have ignored its rasping even for a few minutes. Sharply he glanced about, trying to determine its source, but it seemed to have none. Whenever he approached a point where it appeared to be loudest, then it would fade or shift, perhaps to the far side of the village.

He tried to imagine what an alien culture would want with a mind-shattering noise—although, of course, it would not necessarily have been unpleasant to them.

He stopped and snapped his fingers as a wild but nevertheless plausible notion entered his mind. Could this be music?

He toyed with the idea, trying to visualize the village as it had been long ago. Here a music-loving people had possibly gone about their daily tasks to the accompaniment of what was to them beautiful strains of melody.

The hideous whistling went on and on, waxing and waning. Jenner tried to put buildings between himself and the sound. He sought refuge in various rooms, hoping that at least one would be soundproof. None were. The whistle followed him wherever he went.

He retreated into the desert, and had to climb halfway up one of the slopes before the noise was low enough not to disturb him. Finally, breathless but immeasurably relieved, he sank down on the sand and thought blankly:

What now?

The scene that spread before him had in it qualities of both heaven and hell. It was all too familiar now—the red sands, the stony dunes, the small, alien village promising so much and fulfilling so little.

Jenner looked down at it with his feverish eyes and ran his parched tongue over his cracked dry lips. He knew that he was a dead man unless he could alter the automatic food-making machines that must be hidden somewhere in the walls and under the floors of the buildings.

In ancient days, a remnant of Martian civilization had survived here in this village. The inhabitants had died off, but the village lived on, keeping itself clean of sand, able to provide refuge for any Martian who might come along. But there were no Martians. There was only Bill Jenner, pilot of the first rocketship ever to land on Mars.

He had to make the village turn out food and drink that he could take. Without tools, except his hands, with scarcely any knowledge of chemistry, he must force it to change its habits.

Tensely he hefted his water bag. He took another sip and fought the same grim fight to prevent himself from guzzling it down to the last drop. And, when he had won the battle once more he stood up and started down the slope.

He could last, he estimated, not more than three days. In that time he must conquer the village.

He was already among the trees when it suddenly struck him that the "music" had stopped. Relieved, he bent over a small shrub, took a good firm hold of it—and pulled.

It came up easily, and there was a slab of marble attached

to it. Jenner stared at it, noting with surprise that he had been mistaken in thinking the stalks came up through a hole in the marble. It was merely stuck to the surface. Then he noticed something else—the shrub had no roots. Almost instinctively, Jenner looked down at the spot from which he had torn the slab of marble along with the plant. There was sand there.

He dropped the shrub, slipped to his knees, and plunged his fingers into the sand. Loose sand trickled through them. He reached deep, using all his strength to force his arm and hand down; sand—nothing but sand.

He stood up and frantically tore up another shrub. It also came up easily, bringing with it a slab of marble. It had no roots, and where it had been was sand.

With a kind of mindless disbelief, Jenner rushed over to a fruit tree and shoved at it. There was a momentary resistance, and then the marble on which it stood split and lifted slowly into the air. The tree fell over with a swish and a crackle as its dry branches and leaves broke and crumbled into a thousand pieces. Underneath where it had been was sand.

Sand everywhere. A city built on sand. Mars, planet of sand. That was not completely true of course. Seasonable vegetation had been observed near the polar ice-caps. All but the hardiest of it died with the coming of summer. It had been intended that the rocketship land near one of those shallow, tideless seas.

By coming down out of control, the ship had wrecked more than itself. It had wrecked the chances for life of the only survivor of the voyage.

Jenner came slowly out of his daze. He had a thought then. He picked up one of the shrubs he had already torn loose, braced his foot against the marble to which it was attached, and tugged, gently at first, then with increasing strength.

It came loose finally, but there was no doubt that the two were part of a whole. The shrub was growing out of the marble.

Marble? Jenner knelt beside one of the holes from which he had torn a slab, and bent over an adjoining section. It was quite porous—calciferous rock, most likely, but not true marble at all. As he reached toward it, intending to break off

a piece, it changed color. Astounded, Jenner drew back.
Around the break, the stone was turning a bright orange-yellow. He studied it uncertainly, then tentatively he touched it.

It was if he had dipped his fingers into searing acid. There
was a sharp, biting, burning pain. With a gasp, Jenner jerked
his hand clear.

The continuing anguish made him feel faint. He swayed
and moaned, clutching the bruised members to his body.
When the agony finally faded and he could look at the injury,
he saw that the skin had peeled and that blood blisters had
formed already. Grimly Jenner looked down at the break in
the stone. The edges remained bright orange-yellow.

The village was alert, ready to defend itself from further
attacks.

Suddenly weary, he crawled into the shade of a tree. There
was only one possible conclusion to draw from what had happened, and it almost defied common sense. This lonely village
was alive.

As he lay there, Jenner tried to imagine a great mass of
living substance growing into the shape of buildings, adjusting
itself to suit another life form, accepting the rôle of servant
in the widest meaning of the term.

If it would serve one race, why not another? If it could adjust to Martians, why not to human beings?

There would be difficulties of course. He guessed wearily
that essential elements would not be available. The oxygen
for water would come from the air ... thousands of compounds could be made from sand. ... Though it meant death
if he failed to find a solution, he fell asleep even as he started
to think about what they might be.

When he woke it was quite dark.

Jenner climbed heavily to his feet. There was a drag to his
muscles that alarmed him. He wet his mouth from his water
bag and staggered toward the entrance of the nearest building. Except for the scraping of his shoes on the "marble," the
silence was intense.

He stopped short, listened, and looked. The wind had died
away. He couldn't see the mountains that rimmed the valley,
but the buildings were still dimly visible, black shadows in a
shadow world.

For the first time, it seemed to him that, in spite of his new
hope, it might be better if he died. Even if he survived, what

had he to look forward to? Only too well he recalled how hard it had been to rouse interest in the trip and to raise the large amount of money required. He remembered the colossal problems that had had to be solved in building the ship, and some of the men who had solved them were buried somewhere in the Martian desert.

It might be twenty years before another ship from Earth would try to reach the only other planet in the Solar System that had shown signs of being able to support life.

During those uncountable days and nights, those years, he would be here alone. That was the most he could hope for— if he lived. As he fumbled his way to a dais in one of the rooms, Jenner considered another problem: How did one let a living village know that it must alter its processes? In a way, it must already have grasped that it had a new tenant. How could he make it realize he needed food in a different chemical combination than that which it had served in the past; that he liked music, but on a different scale system; and that he could use a shower each morning—of water, not of poison gas?

He dozed fitfully, like a man who is sick rather than sleepy. Twice he wakened, his lips on fire, his eyes burning, his body bathed in perspiration. Several times he was startled into consciousness by the sound of his own harsh voice crying out in anger and fear at the night.

He guessed, then, that he was dying.

He spent the long hours of darkness tossing, turning, twisting, befuddled by waves of heat. As the light of morning came, he was vaguely surprised to realize that he was still alive. Restlessly he climbed off the dais and went to the door.

A bitingly cold wind blew, but it felt good to his hot face. He wondered if there was enough pneumococci in his blood for him to catch pneumonia. He decided not.

In a few moments he was shivering. He retreated back into the house, and for the first time noticed that, despite the doorless doorway, the wind did not come into the building at all. The rooms were cold but not draughty.

That started an association: Where had this terrible body heat come from? He teetered over to the dais where he spent the night. Within seconds he was sweltering in a temperature of about one hundred and thirty.

He climbed off the dais, shaken by his own stupidity. He

estimated that he had sweated at least two quarts of moisture out of his dried-up body on that furnace of a bed.

This village was not for human beings. Here even the beds were heated for creatures who needed temperatures far beyond the heat comfortable for men.

Jenner spent most of the day in the shade of a large tree. He felt exhausted, and only occasionally did he even remember that he had a problem. When the whistling started, it bothered him at first, but he was too tired to move away from it. There were long periods when he hardly heard it, so dulled were his senses.

Late in the afternoon he remembered the shrubs and the trees he had torn up the day before and wondered what had happened to them. He wet his swollen tongue with the last few drops of water in his bag, climbed lackadaisically to his feet, and went to look for the dried-up remains.

There weren't any. He couldn't even find the holes where he had torn them out. The living village had absorbed the dead tissue into itself and had repaired the breaks in its "body."

That galvanised Jenner. He began to think again ... about mutations, genetic readjustments, life forms adapting to new environments. There'd been lectures on that before the ship left Earth, rather generalized talks designed to acquaint the explorers with the problems men might face on an alien planet. The important principle was quite simple: adjust or die.

The village had to adjust to him. He doubted if he could seriously damage it, but he could try. His own need to survive must be placed on as sharp and hostile a basis as that.

Frantically Jenner began to search his pockets. Before leaving the rocket he had loaded himself with odds and ends of small equipment. A jack-knife, a folding metal cup, a printed radio, a tiny superbattery that could be charged by spinning an attached wheel—and for which he had brought along, among other things, a powerful electric fire lighter.

Jenner plugged the lighter into the battery and deliberately scraped the red-hot end along the surface of the "marble." The reaction was swift. The substance turned an angry purple this time. When an entire section of the floor had changed color, Jenner headed for the nearest stall trough, entering far enough to activate it.

There was a noticeable delay. When the food finally flowed into the trough, it was clear that the living village had realized the reason for what he had done. The food was a pale, creamy color, where earlier it had been a murky gray.

Jenner put his finger into it but withdrew it with a yell and wiped his finger. It continued to sting for several moments. The vital question was: Had it deliberately offered him food that would damage him, or was it just trying to appease him without knowing what he could eat?

He decided to give it another chance, and entered the adjoining stall. The gritty stuff that flooded up this time was yellower. It didn't burn his finger, but Jenner took one taste and spat it out. He had the feeling that he had been offered a soup made of a greasy mixture of clay and petrol.

He was thirsty now with a need heightened by the unpleasant taste in his mouth. Desperately he rushed outside and tore open the water bag, seeking the wetness inside. In his fumbling eagerness, he spilled a few precious drops on to the courtyard. Down he went on his face and licked them up.

Half a minute later, he was still licking, and there was still water.

The fact penetrated suddenly. He raised himself and gazed wonderingly at the droplets of water that sparkled on the smooth stone. As he watched, another one squeezed up from the apparently solid surface and shimmered in the light of the sinking sun.

He bent, and with the tip of his tongue sponged up each visible drop. For a long time he lay with his mouth pressed to the "marble," sucking up the tiny bits of water that the village doled out to him.

The glowing white sun disappeared behind a hill. Night fell, like the dropping of a black screen. The air turned cold, then icy. He shivered as the wind keened through his ragged clothes. But what finally stopped him was the collapse of the surface from which he had been drinking.

Jenner lifted himself in surprise, and in the darkness gingerly felt over the stone. It had genuinely crumbled. Evidently the substance had yielded up its available water and had disintegrated in the process. Jenner estimated that he had drunk altogether an ounce of water.

It was a convincing demonstration of the willingness of the village to please him, but there was another, less satisfying implication. If the village had to destroy part of itself every time it gave him a drink, then clearly the supply was not unlimited.

Jenner hurried inside the nearest building, climbed on to a dais—and climbed off again hastily, as the heat blazed up at him. He waited, to give the Intelligence a chance to realize he wanted a change, then lay down once more. The heat was as great as ever.

He gave that up because he was too tired to persist and too sleepy to think of a method that might let the village know he needed a different bedroom temperature. He slept on the floor with an uneasy conviction that it could *not* sustain him for long. He woke up many times during the night and thought, "Not enough water. No matter how hard it tries—" Then he would sleep again, only to wake once more, tense and unhappy.

Nevertheless, morning found him briefly alert; and all his steely determination was back—that iron will-power that had brought him at least five hundred miles across an unknown desert.

He headed for the nearest trough. This time, after he had activated it, there was a pause of more than a minute; and then about a thimbleful of water made a wet splotch at the bottom.

Jenner licked it dry, then waited hopefully for more. When none came he reflected gloomily that somewhere in the village an entire group of cells had broken down and released their water for him.

Then and there he decided that it was up to the human being, who could move around, to find a new source of water for the village, which could not move.

In the interim, of course, the village would have to keep him alive, until he had investigated the possibilities. That meant, above everything else, he must have some food to sustain him while he looked around.

He began to search his pockets. Towards the end of his food supply, he had carried scraps and pieces wrapped in small bits of cloth. Crumbs had broken off into the pocket, and he had searched for them often during those long days in the desert. Now, by actually ripping the seams, he discovered tiny particles of meat and bread, little bits of grease and other unidentifiable substances.

Carefully he leaned over the adjoining stall and placed the scrapings in the trough there. The village would not be able to offer him more than a reasonable facsimile. If the spilling of a few drops on the courtyard could make it aware of his need for water, then a similar offering might give it the clue it needed as to the chemical nature of the food he could eat.

Jenner waited, then entered the second stall and activated it. About a pint of thick, creamy substance trickled into the bottom of the trough. The smallness of the quantity seemed evidence that perhaps it contained water.

He tasted it. It had a sharp, musty flavor and a stale odor. It was almost as dry as flour—but his stomach did not reject it.

Jenner ate slowly, acutely aware that at such moments as this the village had him at its mercy. He could never be sure that one of the food ingredients was not a slow-acting poison.

When he had finished the meal he went to a food trough in another building. He refused to eat the food that came up. but activated still another trough. This time he received a few drops of water.

He had come purposefully to one of the tower buildings. Now he started up the ramp that led to the upper floor. He paused only briefly in the room he came to, as he had already discovered that they seemed to be additional bedrooms. The familiar dais was there in a group of three.

What interested him was that the circular ramp continued to wind on upward. First to another, smaller room that seemed to have no particular reason for being. Then it wound on up to the top of the tower, some seventy feet above the ground. It was high enough for him to see beyond the rim of all the surrounding hilltops. He had thought it might be, but he had been too weak to make the climb before. Now he looked out to every horizon. Almost immediately the hope that had brought him up faded.

The view was immeasurably desolate. As far as he could see was an arid waste, and every horizon was hidden in a mist of wind-blown sand.

Jenner gazed with a sense of despair. If there were a Martian sea out there somewhere, it was beyond his reach.

Abruptly he clenched his hands in anger against his fate, which seemed inevitable now. At the very worse, he had hoped he would find himself in a mountainous region. Seas and mountains were generally the two main sources of water. He should have known, of course, that there were very few mountains on Mars. It would have been a wild coincidence if he had actually run into a mountain range.

His fury faded because he lacked the strength to sustain any emotion. Numbly he went down the ramp.

His vague plan to help the village ended as swiftly and finally as that.

His days drifted by, but as to how many he had no idea. Each time he went to eat, a smaller amount of water was doled out to him. Jenner kept telling himself that each meal would have to be his last. It was unreasonable for him to expect the village to destroy itself when his fate was certain now.

What was worse, it became increasingly clear that the food was not good for him. He had misled the village as to his needs by giving it stale, perhaps even tainted, samples, and prolonged the agony for himself. At times after he had eaten Jenner felt dizzy for hours. All too frequently his head ached and his body shivered with fever.

The village was doing what it could. The rest was up to him, and he couldn't even adjust to an approximation of Earth food.

For two days he was too sick to drag himself to one of the troughs. Hour after hour he lay on the floor. Some time during the second night the pain in his body grew so terrible that he finally made up his mind.

"If I can get to a dais," he told himself, "the heat alone will kill me; and in absorbing my body, the village will get back some of its lost water."

He spent at least an hour crawling laboriously up the ramp of the nearest dais, and when he finally made it, he lay as one already dead. His last waking thought was: "Beloved friends, I'm coming."

The hallucination was so complete that momentarily he seemed to be back in he control room of the rocketship, and all around him were his former companions.

With a sigh of relief Jenner sank into a dreamless sleep.

He woke to the sound of a violin. It was a sad, sweet music that told of the rise and fall of a race long dead.

Jenner listened for a while and then, with abrupt excitement, realized the truth. This was a substitute for the whistling—the village had adjusted its music to him!

Other sensory phenomena stole in upon him. The dais felt comfortably warm, not hot at all. He had a feeling of wonderful physical well-being.

Eagerly he scrambled down the ramp to the nearest food stall. As he crawled forward, his nose close to the floor, the trough filled with a steamy mixture. The odor was so rich and pleasant that he plunged his face into it and slopped it up greedily. It had the flavor of thick, meaty soup and was warm and soothing to his lips and mouth. When he had eaten it all, for the first time he did not need a drink of water.

"I've won!" thought Jenner. "The village has found a way!"

After a while he remembered something and crawled to the bathroom. Cautiously, watching the ceiling, he eased himself backward into the shower stall. The yellowish spray came down, cool and delightful.

Ecstatically Jenner wriggled his four-foot tail and lifted his long snout to let the thin streams of liquid wash away the food impurities that clung to his sharp teeth.

Then he waddled out to bask in the sun and listen to the timeless music.

a can of paint

THE landing jets worked like a dream. The small machine settled gently on an open meadow in a long, shallow, brilliantly green valley. A few minutes later, the first man of earth ever to set foot on Venus stepped gingerly down and stood on the lush grass beside his cigar-shaped spaceship.

Kilgour drew a deep, slow breath. The air was like wine, a little high in oxygen content, but tingingly sweet and fresh and warm. He had a sudden conviction that he had come to paradise. He pulled out his notebook, and wrote down the impression. Any thoughts like that would be worth gold when he got back to Earth. And he would darn well need the money, too.

He finished the writing, and he was putting away his notebook, when he saw the cube.

It was lying on its side on the grass in a slight indentation, as if it had fallen from something not very high. It was a translucent crystalline block with a handle. It was about eight inches square, and it shone with a dull luster like ivory. It seemed to have no purpose.

Kilgour brought some energy testers from the ship, and touched various parts of the crystal with the wire ends. Electricity: negative; electronic: negative. It was not radio-active, nor did it respond to any of the acids he used. It refused to conduct a current of electricity, and likewise rejected the more feverish advances of the electronic enveloper. He put on a rubber glove, and touched the handle. Nothing happened. He slid his gloved fingers caressingly over the cube, and finally gripped the handle tightly. Still there was no response.

Kilgour hesitated. Then tugged at the thing. It lifted easily; its weight he estimated at about four pounds. He set it down again and, stepping back, surveyed it. A slow excitement was starting in his brain. It tingled down to his toes as he realized what was here.

The cube was a manufactured article. There was intelligent life on Venus. He had spent a dreary year in space, wondering, hoping, dreaming about that. And here was evidence. Venus was inhabited.

Kilgour whirled towards the ship. Have to search for a city, he thought tensely. It didn't matter any more if he wasted fuel. Replacements were now possible. He was still in the act of turning, when he saw the cube out of the corner of his eyes. His enthusiasm suffered a pause.

What was he going to do with it? It would be foolish to leave it here. Once departed from this valley, he might never find it again. He'd be wise, though, to be careful about what he took aboard his ship. Suppose the cube had been left there for him to find?

The idea seemed fantastic, and some of his doubts faded. A couple more tests, he decided, and then—He took off his glove, and gingerly touched the handle with his bare finger.

"I contain paint!" something said into his mind.

Kilgour jumped backward. "Hug!" he gulped.

He looked around wildly. But he was alone in a green valley that stretched into distance. He returned his attention to the crystal block. Again, he touched the handle.

"I contain paint." This time there was no doubt. The thought was clear and sharp in his mind.

Kilgour straightened slowly. He stood, mentally dazzled, staring at his find. It took a long moment to start his thought on the uphill climb of imagining the technological stature of a race that could turn out such a container. His mind soared, and then reluctantly retreated. He grew amazed. Because, simple though it was, nothing in the science of man even foreshadowed such a development. A container of paint that said—what it had said. A can labeled with a self-identifying thought.

Kilgour began to grin. His long, homely face twisted with good humor. His gray-green eyes lighted up. His lips parted, revealing even, white teeth. He laughed joyously. A can of paint! The paint would probably have other ingredients than white lead, linseed oil, and a coloring oxide. But that was something to explore later.

For the moment, possession was enough. No matter what else he discovered on Venus, his trip was already paid for. It was the simple, used-every-day things that made fortunes.

Briskly, Kilgour reached down, grabbed the handle with his bare hand, and started to lift.

He had got it off the ground, when a dazzlingly bright liquid squirted from it on to his chest. It spread quickly over his body, clinging like glue, yet running swiftly. It was white when it started, but it changed to red, yellow, blue, violet, then it spread into a myriad of shades. He stood finally, drenched clothes flashing all the colors of the rainbow. And at first he was furious rather than alarmed.

He began to strip. He was wearing a pullover sweat shirt and a pair of sport shorts; nothing else. The two pieces sparkled like varicolored fire as, with a synchronized jerk he unloosened his belt and pulled the shirt up over his head.

He could feel the liquid running down over his bare body; and it was not until he had removed his shirt—his shorts had fallen around his ankles—that he noticed an odd fact. The paint, which had been mostly on his shirt, had flowed completely off it and on to his skin. Not a drop had fallen to the ground. And his shorts were clean also.

All the paint was on his body. It glowed as it thinned out over the greater surface. It sparkled and shimmered like a flame seen through a prism as he wiped at it with his shirt. But it didn't come off. Frowning, he pushed at it with his hands. It clung to his fingers with a warm stickiness. It bobbed and danced with color as he shoved it groundward. It went down one place, and came up another.

It was a unit, of which no portion would separate from any other portion. It flowed so far, then no farther. It assumed every conceivable shape. But always it remained one piece. Like a vivid, tinted, immensely flexible shawl draped in various patterns, it altered its form, not its essential oneness. After ten minutes, he was still no nearer getting rid of it.

" 'Paint'," Kilgour read aloud out of his medical book, " 'can be removed by applying turpentine'."

There was turpentine in his storeroom. He secured the bottle, and climbed out of the ship again, he poured a generous measure into the cupped palm of his hand, and applied it vigorously. That is, he started to apply it. The turpentine flowed out of his hand and on to the ground. The paint wouldn't allow itself to be touched by the liquid.

It took several attempts to convince the astounded Kilgour But finally, still determined, he re-entered the ship. In quick succession he tried petrol, water, wine, even some of his precious rocket fuel. The paint wouldn't make contact with any of them. He stepped under a shower. The water rained down on the portion of his body that was covered by paint, a fine stinging spray of wetness. But there was no sensation at all where the paint clung.

And it definitely didn't wash off.

He filled his bathtub, and seated himself in it. The paint shinnied up his neck, and around his chin, and flowed over his mouth and nose. It didn't go in his nostrils or his mouth, but it covered both apertures. Kilgour stopped breathing, and sat stubborn; then he saw the paint was creeping up towards his eyes. He jumped out of the tub and ducked his head into the water.

The paint retreated from his nose, hesitated at his mouth, and then sank back halfway towards the lower end of his chin. It seemed to find some anchor point there for, no matter how deep or how often he ducked, it refused to go any lower.

Apparently, having reached his head, it was not prepared to give up that vantage point. Kilgour spread a rubber mat on his favorite chair and sat down to do some hard thinking. The whole incident was ridiculous. He'd be the laughing stock of the solar system if it was ever found out that he had got himself into such a fantastic predicament.

By some accident, a can of Venusian paint had been dropped or lost on this uninhabited meadow; and here he was, smeared with the stuff. The quick way it had flowed over his mouth and nose showed that thought-mindless, it could be deadly. Suppose it had refused to retreat an inch. He would have suffocated in a few minutes and would now be lying dead in his bathtub.

Kilgour felt a chill climb his spine. The chill remained even after it struck him that he could easily have forced a funnel into his mouth, and breathed that way. The chill remained because it was only accident that the incredible stuff hadn't climbed up over his eyes.

He pictured a blind suffocating man searching in a roomy storeroom for a funnel.

It took a long minute for his normally sunny disposition to make a partial comeback. He sat stiff, forcing his mind. Paint—that jumped out of a can, showed no sign of drying, yet wasn't really a liquid, because it wouldn't soak into clothing or flow according to the law of gravity. And wouldn't let liquid touch it.

Kilgour's mind paused there, in sudden comprehension. Why, of course. Waterproof. He should have remembered. This was no ordinary paint. It was waterproof, rainproof, liquidproof—the ultimate paint.

He grew excited. He stood up jerkily, and began to pace the floor. For twenty-five years, ever since the first of the super rockets had gushed out to the barren Moon and then to semibarren Mars, Venus had been the goal of the explorers. Journeys there, however, had been forbidden until some means was discovered to overcome the danger of the ships falling into the Sun. That incandescent fate had befallen two ships. And it had been mathematically proven, not merely by cranks, that such a catastrophe would happen to every spaceship until the planets Earth and Venus attained a certain general position with relation to each other and Jupiter.

The ideal conditions were not due to occur for another twenty eight years. But six months before Kilgour took off, a famous astronomer had pointed out that some of the conditions would prevail for about a year. The article caused a sensation among spacemen; and, though the goverment refused to withdraw its ban, Kilgour had heard that a high patrol officer had privately stated that he would look the other way if anybody started out. And that he would see to it that men of like mind carried out the necessary pre-flight inspections. Several expeditions, ostensibly bound for Mars, had been busily fitting up when Kilgour launched his small craft into space, Venusbound.

Great things were expected of Venus. But not so great as this. Kilgour stopped his pacing. A race that could develop a perfect paint, *anything* perfect, was going to prove worth knowing.

His thought ended. He had glanced down at his body. And now, he saw something that startled him. The paint, brilliant in its million facets of changing color, was spreading. In the beginning, it had covered a quarter of his flesh. Now, it covered a good third. If it kept on, it would soon overrun him from head to toe, eyes and ears and nose and mouth and all.

It was time he started figuring ways and means of removal. In earnest.

Kilgour wrote:

"A perfect paint should be waterproof and weatherproof as well as beautiful. It should also be easily removable."

He stared gloomily at the final sentence. And then, in a fit of temper, he flung down the pencil and walked over to the bathroom mirror. He peered into it with a nasty smirk on his face.

"Pretty, aren't you!" he snarled at his blazing image. "Like a gipsy arrayed in dance finery."

The reality, he saw on second glance, was more chromatically splendid than that. He shone in about ninety colors. The various combinations did not blur dully one into the other. They merged with a sharp brightness that seemed to make even the most subtle shades project with intensity. Yet in some curious fashion the paint was not showy. It was bright, but it did not hurt his eyes. It was brilliant, but it failed to jar his sense of good taste. He had come to sneer, but he remained several minutes to appraise its startling beauty.

He turned away at last. "If," he thought, "I could get a spoonful loose, I could put it into a retort and analyse it."

But he had tried that. He tried it again, with a sudden hope. As before, the paint flowed into the spoon willingly, but when he raised the spoon, it flowed back on to his skin. Kilgour procured a knife, and tried to hold the paint on his spoon. But when he lifted his hand, the paint slid between the blade and the spoon like so much oil.

Kilgour decided that his strength was not sufficient to press the knife tight on to the spoon edge. He headed for the storeroom. There was a small scoop there with a pressure cover. It was too round and too small; he could only force a little bit of the paint into it. And it took more than a minute to tighten the cover nuts with a wrench. But when he lifted the scoop and opened it, there was a little pool of paint filling the bottom quarter of the scoop.

Kilgour walked over and sat down hastily in his chair. He had the curious, wretched feeling that he was going to be ill. His brain reeled with relief; and it was several minutes before he could even think about his next move. Logically, of course, he ought to remove painstakingly, and it would be painstaking, all the paint by the method he had just evolved.

But first—He poured the paint in the scoop into a measuring retort. It measured just a little more than a dessertspoonful.

There were, he estimated, at least five hundred such spoonfuls on his body, and it would take him—he removed a second scoopful, timing himself—a fraction over two minutes for each operation.

One thousand minutes! Seventeen hours! Kilgour smiled ruefully, and went into the galley. He'd need food four or five times during such a period of time, and right now was one of the times. While he was eating, he pondered the problem with the calmness of a man who has found a solution, and who, therefore, can afford to consider other possibilities.

Seventeen hours was a long time. Surely, now that he had some free paint, he could go into his small chemical lab and quickly discover a dozen chemical reactions that would remove the entire mess from him in a few minutes.

Perhaps a larger, more complete laboratory might have yielded results. His was too small. The paint refused to react to any of the elements and solutions that he had. It wouldn't mix. It wouldn't combine. It wouldn't burn. It was immune to acids and metals, and it did not seem to influence anything he used either catalytically or otherwise.

The paint was inert.

"Of course," Kilgour said at last, explosively, to himself. "How could I have forgotten? The stuff would be weatherproof with a capital W. It's perfect paint."

He went to work with the scoop. He developed a dexterity with the wrench in screwing and unscrewing the nuts, that enabled him to remove a spoonful every three-quarters of a minute. He was so intent on maintaining the speed of the operation that he had half a pailful of paint before it struck him with a tremendous shock that there was still as much paint as ever on his body.

Kilgour trembled with the thought that came. Feverishly, he measured the paint in the half-filled pail. And there was no question. He had emptied into the pail approximately as much as the original crystal container had squirted on to him—without affecting the quantity on his body.

Once applied, the ultimate paint was self-renewing.

He wrote that down at the bottom of his list of the paint's qualities. Then he grew aware that he was perspiring freely. The sweat stood out in little foamy globules over the unpainted part of his body. Kilgour's brain performed its newest leap of comprehension. He snatched up his notebook and jotted down: "The perfect paint is also cold and heatproof."

Within half an hour, it was impossible to be objective about it. The paint covered nearly half his body. His hard work had warmed him considerably. He was roasting from his own animal heat. And scared. He thought shakily: "I've got to get out of here. I've got to find a Venusian city, and get an antidote for this stuff."

It didn't matter any more whether he was made ridiculous or not.

In a spasm of panic, he headed for the control board. His hand reached for the launching lever. But paused at the last instant.

The can! It had said: "I contain paint." Surely it would also have directions for use of contents, and for subsequent removal.

"I'm a pie-eyed nut," Kilgour whispered to himself as he ran. "I should have thought of that ages ago."

The crystal "can" lay on the grass, where he had left it. He snatched at it. "I contain a quarter of paint," it thought at him.

So he had squirted three-quarters of the contents on to himself. It was an important thing to know. He'd be wise not to add the rest to the spreading horror that was enveloping him in an air-tight casing of liquid brilliance.

Cautiously, taking care not to lift the container from the ground, he fumbled over it with his bare hands. Almost instantly, he had his first response. "Directions: Fix controllers around area to be painted, then apply. Paint will dry as soon as controlled area is covered. To remove, press darkener over paint for one terad." The incomprehensible word seemed to refer to a short period of time. "Note," the thought continued, "darkeners may be purchased at your neighborhood hardware and paint stores."

Kilgour thought furiously, "Isn't that just dandy. I'll run over right now, and get me one."

In spite of his seathing words, he felt amazingly better. It was a practical world he had come to, not a nightmare planet where creatures with ten eyes and eight legs moaned and yammered with instant alien hatred for human explorers. People who used paint wouldn't murder him out of hand.

That had been obvious all the time. Intelligence implied a semi-rational outlook, an orderly, organized universe. Naturally, not all non-human races would like human beings. But then, human beings had a habit of not liking each other.

If the container and the paint it contained were criterions, the civilization of Venus was superior to that of man. Accordingly, the inhabitants would be above petty persecution. The fantastic, ludicrous mess he had gotten himself into was basically solved by that fact.

But that didn't stop him from getting hotter and hotter under his coat of paint. It was time he found himself a Venusian. He picked up the container, lifting it with his fingers from underneath. It thought at him:

"Ingredients of this paint, as per government requirements, are:

!?!?!—7%

?!?!?—13%

Liquid light—80% "

"Liquid what?" asked Kilgour aloud.

"Warning," came the thought. "This paint must not be allowed in proximity to volatile substances."

There was no explanation for that, though Kilgour waited for further thoughts. Apparently Venusians knew enough about their government regulations to obey them without question. He himself had tried to put the paint in contact with the volatile substances, turpentine, gasoline, his rocket fuel, and a couple of other explosives. And no harm done. It seemed a silly regulation if it didn't mean anything.

Kilgour set the can down, and headed once more for the control board. The launching lever was glass smooth to his palm as he pulled it back until it clicked. He sat braced, waiting for the automatic machinery to set off the potent violence of fired tubes.

Nothing happened.

Kilgour had a premonition. He jerked the launching lever back into place, then clicked it again. And still there was no explosion.

His brain was reeling. The premonition was a living force. His whole body was heavy with the strength of it. He had poured the rocket fuel back into its great tank after trying to wipe the paint off his flesh with it. It had only been a few litres, but spacemen practised queer economies. He had poured it back because the paint had not seemed to affect it in any way.

"Warning," the can had said. "This paint must not be allowed in proximity to volatile substances."

The inert stuff must have de-energized the eighteen thousand gallons in his one remaining fuel tank.

Try the radio again. He had started sending out signals when he was a few million miles from Venus, and had listend on his receiver. But the great void had remained unresponsive. Nevertheless, the Venusians *must* have such a thing. Surely they would answer an emergency call.

But they didn't. Half an hour went by, and his calls went unheeded. His receiver remained silent, not even static came in on any wave length. He was alone in a universe of choking, crowding, growing, maddening by colorful paint.

Darkener—liquid light—Perhaps it shone, not only in bright exterior light, so that if he turned off the lights—His finger on the switch, he noticed for the first time how dark it was outside. His lock doors were open; and slowly, Kilgour walked over to them and stared out into a night that was unbroken by starlight. The darkness, now that it had come, was intense. The clouds, of course, the eternal clouds of Venus—So bright was the sun at Venus' distance from it that in daytime the clouds were a protection that yet failed to more than dim the dazzling glare.

Now, at night, it was different. The clouds enclosed the planet like the walls and ceiling of a dark room. There was light, naturally. No planet near a sun or in the starry universe could be absolutely shut off from light and energy. His seleniometer would probably be registering well down into the hundred thousandths. Kilgour brought his gaze down from the sky, and saw that the ground was brilliant with the light from his paint. Startled, he stepped out of the door, away from the interior light pouring out of the door of his ship. In the darkness to one side, his body glowed like a multiflamed but meaningless sign. He was so bright he lighted up the grass with patterns of dazzling color. He would be beautiful in death.

He pictured himself sprawled on the floor, covered from head to foot with paint. Eventually the Venusians would find him on this lonely meadow. Perhaps they would wonder what he was, where he had come from. It seemed obvious that they had no interplanetary travel.

Or had they? Kilgour's mind paused momentarily in its feverish gyrations. Was it possible the Venusians had deliberately refrained from making contact with human beings on earth?

His brain couldn't concentrate on anything so unimportant. He went back into the ship. There was something, he was thinking, something he had been intending to do—he couldn't remember, unless it was the radio. He switched it on. Then jumped jerkily as a mechanical voice came through:

"Earthman," it said, "are you there? Earthman, are you there?"

Kilgour clawed at the broadcaster. "Yes," he shouted finally. "Yes, I'm here. And in an awful mess. You must come out at once."

"We know your predicament," said the flat-toned voice, "But we have no intention of rescuing you."

"Huh!" said Kilgour blankly.

"The container of paint," the voice went on, "was dropped from an invisible ship at the door of your machine a few moments after you landed. For some thousands of years we, whom you call Venusians, have watched with considerable uneasiness the development of civilization on the third planet of this sun system. Our people are not adventurous, nor is there a single war known to our recorded history. This is not to say that the struggle for survival has not been a bitter one. But we have an immensely more sluggish metabolism. Long ago our psychologists decided that space flight was not for us.

"We have accordingly concentrated on the development of the purely Venusian way of life, so that when your ship approached our atmosphere, we were confronted with the necessity of deciding under what conditions we would establish relations with human beings. Our decision was to place the container of paint where you would find it. If you had failed to become entangled in the paint, we would have found some other method of testing you.

"Yes, you have heard correctly. You have been, and are being tested. It seems you are failing the test, which is regrettable because it means that all people of your intelligence level or less will be barred from Venus. It has been very difficult to prepare tests for an alien race. And therefore, unless you can think your way through the test, you must die, so that others who come after you may be given that or similar tests without knowing they are being tested, a prime requisite, it seems to us. Our intention is to find a human being who can solve the test we give him, after which we shall examine him with our instruments, and use the results as a measure for future visitors to Venus. All those whose intelligence is the same or higher than that of the successful candidate may come to our planet at will. Such is our unalterable determination.

"The person tested must also be able to leave Venus without help from us. You will readily see why that is necessary. Later, we shall help human beings to improve their spaceships. We are talking to you on a mechanical voice machine. The simple thoughts of the container were very laboriously impressed upon it by a complicated thought machine. It is so very difficult to establish communication with a non-Venusian brain. But now, goodbye. And though this may sound strange, good luck still."

There was a click. All Kilgour's juggling with the dials produced no further sound.

He sat, all the ship's lights switched off, waiting for death. It was not a quiescent wait. His whole being palpitated with the will to live. A darkener! What in the name of the ebony gods could it be?

The question was not new to Kilgour. For an hour he had sat in a room made fantastic by the blaze of color from his painted body. He sat with his notebook, frantically going over the data he had.

A perfect paint made of—eighty per cent liquid light. Light was light; the liquid must follow the same laws as the beam. Or must it? And what of it? A perfect paint capable of—his mind refused to go through the list of qualities again. He felt physically ill, and time and again he fought off nausea.

He was so hot, it was like a fever. His feet dangled in a pan of cold water; the theory of that had been that if his blood had a cold area to run through, it wouldn't start boiling.

Actually, he knew that there was little danger of his temperature rising beyond its present almost unbearable point. There was such a thing as a limit to animal heat, particularly

since it had penetrated at last that he had better stick to vita-
min capsules and leave calories alone. It would be insane to
take in fuel that manufactured body heat. The gravest danger
was that with his body overrun by the paint, his pores would
be unable to breathe. Death would follow, how quickly Kilgour didn't know.

His ignorance didn't add to his peace of mind. Funny,
though, that now he was reluctantly waiting for death, it was
slow in coming. The thought jarred Kilgour out of his developing incoherence. Slow? He leaped to his feet. Because it
was slow. He raced for the bathroom mirror. In a dizzy excitement he peered at his image.

The paint still covered only half his body. It had not expanded during the past hour. *The past hour, during which he
had sat in darkness except for the light from the paint.*

The paint, he noted more critically, had not lost ground. It
still covered half his body. But, actually, that was natural. It
was made to survive the black Venusian night. Suppose, however, that he climbed into the greater darkness of his in-
sulated-against energy, empty fuel tank?

For half an hour Kilgour sat in the tank; and then
climbed out again, shaky but still determined. Absolute
darkness must be the solution, but he was missing something
vital. It seemed obvious that if darkness alone was enough,
then the fuel in his full fuel tank would by this time have
cleared itself of the effects of the paint. He tried the
launcher; and there was no explosion. There must be something else.

"The problem," thought Kilgour, "is to drain off the eighty
percent liquid light by providing a sufficient darkness, or by
some other means. But it's almost impossible for darkness to
be darker than it is inside that tank. It's insulated against outside energies. So what's wrong?"

The insulation! That was it. The light from the paint
merely reflected from the walls, and was re-absorbed by the
paint. There was no place for the light to escape. Solution:
Remove the insulation.

No, that was wrong. Kilgour's excitement sagged. With the
insulation removed, the light would escape all right, but the
outside energies would seep in to replace the escaped quantity. Better test that, though.

He did. And it was so. He came out as covered with paint

as ever. He was standing there, in the grip of hopelessness, when the answer struck him.

On the way back to Earth a month later, Kilgour ran into the radio signals of another ship approaching Venus. He explained what had happened. He finished, "So you'll have no difficulty landing. The Venusians will give you the keys to their colorful cities."

"But just a minute!" came the puzzled reply. "I thought you said they'll only allow people whose intelligence is the same as, or greater than, that of the person who succeeds in their test. You must be quite a bright lad to have done so. But we're only a bunch of dumb spacemen. So where does that leave us?"

"You're sitting right on top of the world," Kilgour responded cheerfully. "And I mean Venus. Like most spacemen, I was never noted for my I.Q. My forte has always been vim, vigor, and a spirit of adventure." He concluded modestly, "Since I'm the measuring rod for admittance, I would say that at a conservative estimate, ninety-nine per cent of the human race can now visit Venus."

"But—"

Kilgour cut him off. "Don't ask me why their test was so simple. Maybe you'll understand when you see them." He frowned. "You're not going to like the Venusians, friend. But one look at their many-legged, multi-armed bodies will give you some idea of what they meant when they said it was difficult to figure out tests for alien minds. And now, any more questions?"

"Yes. How *did* you get rid of that paint?"

Kilgour grinned. "Photocells and barium salt. I took a bank of photo-converter cells and a barium battery into the tank with me. They absorbed the light from the paint. The rest, a fine, brownish dust, settled on to the floor; and I was a free man. I reenergized the rocket fuel the same way."

He laughed joyously. "Toodleoo! Be seeing you. I've got a cargo aboard that must be marketed."

"A cargo! Of what?"

"Paint. Thousands of cans of gorgeous paint. Earth shall in beauty live for evermore. And I've got the exclusive agency."

The two ships passed in the night of space, on to their separate destinations.

defense

IN the bowels of the dead planet, tired old machinery stirred. Pale tubes flickered with uneven life, and slowly, reluctantly, a main switch was wheezed out of its negative into its positive position.

There was a hissing and a fusing of metal as the weary copper alloy sagged before a surge of mighty power. The metal stiffened like human muscles subjected to the intolerable shock of electric current, and then with a lurch the switch dissolved in flame and settled with a thud into the dust of an unswept floor.

But before it died it succeeded in starting a wheel turning.

The texture of the ancient silence of the chamber was changed now. The wheel spun lazily on a scabrous cushion of oil that, sealed off as it had been, had survived a million years. Three times the wheel made its rounds, and then its support crumbled to the floor. The shapeless mass that had been a wheel ended up against a wall, half powder and all useless.

Before it died, the wheel spun a shaft that opened a tiny hole at the bottom of a pile of uranium. In the passageway below the hole, other uranium gleamed a dull silvery brightness.

With a cosmic breathlessness, the two piles of metal regarded each other. They stirred. The life that flowed between them needed no gestation period. One look, and they changd to a fiery activity. What had been solid metal liquefied. The upper flushed down upon the lower.

The flaming mass cascaded along a channel and into a special chamber. There, coiling back upon itself, it simmered and seethed, and waited. It warmed those cold, insulated walls, and that set off an electric current. The fateful current pulsed silently through the caves of a dead world.

In all the chambers of an interlocking system of underground forts, voices spoke. The messages whispered hoarsely from receivers, in a language so long forgotten that even the echoes mocked the meaning. In a thousand rooms, voices from an incredibly remote past spoke into the silence, waited for response and, receiving none, accepted that mindless stillness as assent.

In a thousand rooms then, switches plunged home, wheels spun, uranium flowed into specially built chambers. There was a pause while a final process ran its course. Electronic machines asked each other wordless questions.

A pointer pointed.

"There?" asked a tube, insistently. "From there?"

The pointer held steady.

The questioning tube, having waited its specified time, closed a relay.

"There," it said positively to a thousand waiting-in-line electronic devices. "The object that is approaching has definitely come from *there!*"

The thousand receptors were calm.

"Ready?" they asked.

In the mechanism chambers behind the seething uranium chambers, lights laconically shrugged their readiness.

The reply was curt, an ultimate command.

"*Fire!*"

When they were five hundred miles from the surface, Peters, pale and intense, turned to Grayson.

"What the hell," he said violently, "was that?"

"What? I wasn't looking."

"I'll swear I saw flashes of fire leap up from down there. So many I couldn't count them. And then I had the impression of something passing us in the dark."

Grayson shook his head pityingly. "So the little boogies have got you at last, pal. Can't take the tension of the first attempt to land on the moon. Relax, boy, relax. We're almost there."

"But I'll swear—"

"Nuts!"

More than 238,000 miles behind them, the earth rocked and shook as a thousand super-atomic bombs exploded in one continuous barrage of mushrooming thunder.

Instantly, the mist spread throughout the stratosphere, blotting out the details of catastrophe from the watching stars.

the rulers

IT was a typical Washington dinner party. Minor political lights adorned at least a dozen chairs. And here and there along the massive table sat men who were of more than satellite importance. One of several inevitable discussions had started near the hostess—that was purely accidental—and the dinner had reached the bored stage where almost everybody was listening with polite attention.

"Science," the plump man was saying, "has made such strides since the war that it's already possible to foresee a time when everything we do, or use in any way, will be either completely artificial, artificially enhanced, supernatural, or better than the original."

The dark-haired man with the quizzical expression shook his head. "If that proves true, it will be because the human race is lazier than I for one believe. Plastics I might concede without argument but with mental reservations. I'll even go so far as to agree that anything which does not directly affect the human body can be made artificially, and it won't matter. But when you come to the body itself—no, sir. Vitamin-enriched foods, for instance, contain only the extra vitamins, but natural foods contain not only the well-known factors such as vitamins, minerals, but also all the as yet unknown factors. Finally, show me even a near substitute for the human brain, and I'll accept your point."

"It isn't so much," said the plump man with satisfaction, "that there is a substitute, but have you perhaps heard of the *h* drug? It's not a brain, but it so modifies the mind's natural impulses that it might be said to create an artificial brain."

At this moment, the hostess showed one of her periodic signs of life.

"*H* drug?" she echoed. "Artificial brain? I know just the man to decide any such question." She turned, and said, "Dr. Latham, will you stop talking for a moment to that perfectly

96

beautiful wife of yours ... you don't mind, Margaret? ... and come to the aid of these poor gentlemen?"

Dr. Latham was a tall, slender man with a lean, sensitive face and quick brown eyes. He laughed. "It just so happens that I heard the argument with one ear."

"And me with the other one, I suppose," his wife pouted.

He grinned at her. "You're not really mad, so don't even try to pretend."

She sighed. "That comes of being married to a psychomedician, a man who can practically read minds."

Latham ignored her blandly. "I think," he began, "I can illustrate the argument very neatly by a case I handled for the government a year ago. . . ."

By half-past eleven, Latham knew that he had found what he had been sent after. It was time, therefore, to dissemble suspicion. He excused himself from his guide, picked up the desk phone of the office they were in, and dialled his hotel.

Miss Segill's face appeared on the screen. "It's you," she said.

Her eyes brightened. Her cheeks thickened with eager laughter lines. Her mouth crinkled. A thousand tiny muscular adjustments transformed her face in one instant from quite receptive attentiveness into a mask of brilliant smile. There were accompanying signals of marked glandular activity, Latham noted, plus a tendency—breathlessness, slight parting of lips, fingering indecisiveness—to a lowering of neutral integration.

Latham studied her appreciatively. He had decided at an early stage of their acquaintanceship to marry this secretary-nurse of his. It was good to know that her love for him rode higher every day. He broke off the thought, and said, "I'll be through here in another half-hour, Miss Segill. Bring your notebook to the little restaurant we saw last night on the way to the hotel—you know the one I mean—and we'll have lunch about 12:15. There won't be much to note down. Got that all?"

"I'll be there," said Miss Segill; then quickly, "Doctor."

Latham paused as he was about to hang up the receiver. The young woman's expression had changed again. The smile was fading now. Replaced by an intent look, crinkled lines between the eyes, a shadow of a forehead frown. Her mouth twitched faintly. Her face lost some of its color. She looked tenser, as if her muscles had stiffened. Anxiety for him intermingled with a tremulous curiosity as to what he had discovered.

"Nothing important, Miss Segill," Latham said. "The whole thing is becoming ridiculous."

He hung up before it occurred to him that she had not actually *asked* the question he had answered. Latham clicked his tongue in self-annoyance. He'd have to watch out for that. His habit of reading people's thoughts and feelings, by a detailed and instantly analyzed understanding of the language of facial and other expressions, would make him seem queer. With his ambitions, he couldn't afford that.

He put the matter temporarily but decisively out of his mind. "Let's go," he said to the guide. "This part of the hospital now, and then I'll be on my way."

"I wouldn't go in there if I were you," the man said in a quiet voice.

"Eh?" said Latham. "Don't be silly. I have to—"

He stopped. The abnormalness of the guide's words struck into him. An ugly thrill trickled up Latham's spine. With a jerk, he turned and stared full at the fellow. Instantly, he realized that he had run across the exception to his ability to comprehend the mind behind the flesh.

The man had been a dull-spoken, mindless nonentity named Godred, or Codred, a creature that said, "And this is the fifteenth floor annex, where we keep patients from Rumania." Or "Main operating room, sir, for the Austrian staff." And said it all without a hint of vascular, muscular, neutral, or cerebral disturbance. He was smiling now, faintly. Where there had been stolidity, intelligence shone like a light replacing darkness. His body lost its heaviness. He straightened, grew perceptibly taller. His lips took on lines of authority. He measured Latham with a sardonic smile. He said:

"We have tolerated your little investigation, doctor, with a mixture of amusement and exasperation. Now we are weary. Go away; depart while you have a whole skin. And don't go through that door."

Latham was thinking: Here was final proof. He'd have to take a look, of course, into the room. After that—His mind wouldn't go that far. He said aloud. "Are you mad? Do you not realize that I represent the United States government?"

The man said, *"Don't go through that door!"*

The door was like the others: a many wooded hardwood combination, beautifully interlaid, and without paint or varnish of any kind. Sandpaper had wrought that miracle finish. It opened at the pressure of Latham's fingers, with only normal resistance. Its threshold held his rigid form for the moment that he stood staring. Then he was running, back the way he had come. The guide grabbed at him. But Latham's movement, his entire reaction, was too quick.

It was as he realized the distance to the nearest exit that he had his first hard shock of fear. Even as he ran, he began to lose hope.

That race along marbled and panelled corridors was like a dream. One of those mad dreams of being pursued. He knew better than to stop. There was a rather long, paved driveway leading to the nearest street. And a taxi was just turning a far corner. He projected his long body and, gasping, succeeded in heading off the taxi. He climbed out five minutes later, waited until the taxi was out of sight, then hailed a second cab. He got off in the depths of heavy downtown traffic, hurried through two monster department stores, and climbed aboard an electair car for the third stage of his bid for escape.

He was calmer now. An intent, rational calmness that included a detailed memory of everything he had said on the phone about where he had told Miss Segill to meet him. He hadn't named the restaurant. It was like consciously dying, then coming to life again, to realize now that he had made that phone call, *and failed to name the restaurant.* They didn't know. They couldn't know. In all this enormous city, they wouldn't be able to locate a café whose name was ". . . You know the one I mean!"

But Miss Segill and he would have to hurry. A quick lunch, then a Taxi-Air to Washington. There wasn't an hour, a minute, to waste.

"I don't understand," Miss Segill said, after he had briefly described his experience. "What *did* you see?"

"Twelve men and a gun."

The girl's eyes remained widened gray-green pools of puzzlement. She shook her head ever so slightly, and her golden curls rippled and shone from the reflected sunlight that poured from the sun cones in the restaurant ceiling.

"Eat your lunch," Latham admonished. "I'll try to make it clear between my own bites. You know the law that was passed, subjecting all hospitals to federal government inspection? The government called it a measure to enforce a uniform hospital service. That reason was a blind, as you know."

Miss Segill nodded wordlessly. Latham went on grimly: "It's real purpose was to find this place. They couldn't conceal anything from me, and they didn't even try. The hospital is crowded with offices and non-sick patients. Naturally, a few offices from which wealthy convalescents could carry on their business, and a few non-sick patients, wouldn't have mattered much. After the war certain European nationalities were barred from the United States unless they came here to see specialists. Even then their activity was restricted. They must go straight to a hospital which had previously agreed to receive them; and, on leaving, head straight for the nearest intercontinental air field.

"It was known that sometimes the visitors had quite a fling seeing American high spots before returning to Europe. But this was tolerated until a very curious suspicion started that at least one of the hundreds of hospitals catering to this old-world traffic was being used as headquarters for something immeasurably bigger. That hospital, which is absolutely crowded *with administration offices* and an almost completely non-sick group of patients, I have now discovered."

"But *what* did you see when you entered that room?"

Latham stared at her grimly. "I saw," he said slowly, "twelve of the thirteen members of the council of the rulers of the world. The thirteenth member was Codred, my guide. I believe they wanted to talk to me, to find out what I knew before killing me. I don't think they expected me to make a break, and that is why I got away. Primarily, I escaped because my mind and eyes are trained to grasp a picture in one-tenth the normal time. Before they could think or act, before they could use the gun that protruded from an instrument board of very futuristic design, actually before they saw me, I had taken my visual photograph and departed. They could have cut me off at the outer door but—"

Latham paused, scowling. Then he shook his head, eyes narrowed. It seemed incredible, now that he had time to think about it, that they had not headed him off. How very sure they must have been. He flicked his gaze uneasily around the fast-filling café and suddenly saw—

"Look!" he hissed. "On the telescreen."

There had been ballet music, and dancers weaving a skillful design on the wall screen. Abruptly, the music ended. The dancers flicked into vagueness. There flashed on to the silvery structure the enormously enlarged faces of Miss Segill and himself. A voice vibrated from the screen:

"Ladies and gentlemen, watch out for this man and woman, believed at this very moment to be in a restaurant having lunch. Their names are Dr. Alexander Latham and Margaret Segill, of Washington, D.C. They are dangerous. Police are authorized to shoot them on sight. That is all."

The music came back on. The images of the dancers resumed their crazy whirling.

It was Latham's inordinately swift observation that saved the moment. At the very instant that other people were beginning to be aware of the screen, he had already seen the two likenesses, and was whispering his commands to Miss Segill.

"Quick, your napkin . . . up to your face . . . hide."

He bent down without waiting for her to act, and began fumbling with his shoelaces. He was down there when the voice delivered its startling sentence of death. After a moment the whole thing seemed impossible. Their names, identities, with no mention of a crime or charge. It indicated police connivance on a scale beyond any previous conception that he had had of danger.

He thought in a spasm of mental agony: They hadn't told him everything at Washington. It was terrible to realize suddenly that he was considered expendable, a bullet fired in dim light in the hope of striking a vaguely seen target.

He was still busy with his shoelaces when Miss Segill leaned forward and said in a strained whisper, "I don't think anybody suspects. But what now?"

Latham had already decided on that. "The phone booths over against the wall," he answered in a low voice. "I have instructions not to phone my reports to Washington, but under the circumstances—"

He broke off. "I'll go first; you follow—into the booth beside mine."

He straightened up, and, dabbing his lips with the napkin, strode to the nearest booth thirty feet away. At the last minute he changed his mind, and paused, his fingers on the catch.

Miss Segill joined him there, "What is it?" she asked.

"Better plan our actions now. And act the moment I've finished phoning. Listen carefully: It doesn't seem possible the police can actually be in on this, but I've reached the point where I trust no one."

"I think we should go straight to the police, and find what's the matter," said Miss Segill, who was now very white, but sounded brave. "After all, we can prove who we are."

"That," said Latham with a cold satisfaction, "is one of the things they expect us to do, I'll warrant. So we won't take the chance. I'll make my phone call, and ask for an escort of air blasts to meet the Taxi-Air we hire. I noticed a Taxi-Air firm a block south of here as I came along."

"What about our lunch bill?"

Latham laughed curtly. "You can't tell me that the cashier or the waitresses have time to pay attention to that telescreen. When we walk past the tables, you be blowing your nose, and I'll start putting on my hat. That should hide our faces to a certain extent—" He broke off, groaned softly, "I wish I had my gun. At least, then I'd be able to put up a fight." He half-turned away from her. "But never mind that. Go into your booth. I'll tap on the aerogel when I'm through."

"I'll pretend," said Miss Segill wanly, "that I'm looking up a number."

Good girl! Latham thought. She was standing up well. Better, it seemed to him, than he would have done in her position. He was inside the booth now. He dialed the key numbers that would connect him with Washington Exchange. The small screen glowed in response. Quickly, Latham dialed the number of the CISA office.

The screen flickered, seemed to have difficulty formulating an image, and then went dead. Latham stared at it, startled. But instantly he dismissed the fear that touched him. The police perhaps; men could always be bought. But not the entire, completely automatic telephone system of a city of a million population. He shook his head, irritated by the fantastic susicion, and redialed his two numbers. This time the screen lit, and stayed lit, and at exactly the right instant the image of a man's head and face formed on it.

"Emergency!" Latham said. "Take this down and—"

He stopped. Then he stared grimly at the sardonic countenance of Codred, who had been his guide at the hospital. The man said mockingly:

"Yes, yes, doctor, go on with your report"—he paused; then hurriedly— "but before you leave the booth please be advised that, once you started running along the corridor, we decided to let you thresh around in our net for a few hours. Your mind will react better to our purpose once it attains that sense of perfect helplessness which we—"

Swiftly as he was speaking, it was still dragging out too long. Talking to gain time, Latham thought. They must have traced the call after the first failure of the phone. Standing there, flashingly picturing the tremendousness of what had already happened, he felt his first terrible fear.

He hung up trembling, backed out of the booth. And then slowly gathered his courage into his body again. He mustered a smile for Miss Segill. But it must have been a sad affair. Her eyes widened.

"You didn't make the call," she said.

Latham didn't have the will to lie to her. "Can't explain now," he said. "We've got to get that Taxi-Air."

He thought again of his gun, this time with a blank dismay. How *could* it have disappeared from his bedroom? No one had been near it. And night marauders might not have the advance knowledge to know that they couldn't enter a psychomedician's room. But they'd know afterward, on the way to jail. Could it be that he had only imagined he had packed it?

He felt better when he reached the street without incident. It seemed to take an unconscionably long time to bridge the gap of one block to the Taxi-Air station. But the very crowds that held them up provided a comforting sense of being unidentifiable. The station was the usual kind. It had a short runway extending over several nearby roofs of business buildings, and an all-aerogel construction, partly transparent, partly translucent, partly white as driven snow.

There were a dozen Taxi-Airs in the lower garage. Latham selected a Packard model he had operated frequently. The driver was reading as they came up, but he put his book away promptly. The man's face twitched as he saw them. The pulse in his neck throbbed visibly. His eyes seemed briefly to reflect more light. He smiled, and said affably:

"Where to, folks?"

"Middle City," Latham said.

He spoke automatically. He had decided on the destination when he was leaving the phone booth, when it was already very clear that anybody heading directly for Washington either by phone or air would be pulled up hard. Actually, now that the driver had reacted as he had, the destination didn't matter.

His plan was simplicity itself. The driver would hold open the door, and let them in. Then he would go around to the other side, and ease himself into the driver's seat. Only that wouldn't happen, Latham calculated. Because *he* would lock the doors as soon as he got inside, dive for the controls, taxi up the winding runway to the roof, and take off. He, Latham—

His thought staggered. Because the driver opened the door, and climbed in himself. From his seat, he grinned. "Climb in, folks," he said.

For an instant, then, the whole business seemed insane. A moment before, the fellow's recognition of them, with its implications, had been something to foil as cleverly as possible. But it was the driver who was handling this situation. And that was amazing. Because he looked so normal, decent, ordinary, a big, easy-going, lumbering chap of about two hundred pounds. The baffling thing was that they had picked this driver by chance, one man of dozens in one of a hundred or more air stations.

With an effort Latham checked the violent swirling of his mind. This was real. Real and deadly and terrible and unmistakable. There was no mistaking the thousand subtle reflexes that showed in the fellow's every movement, every expression. The driver was one of them. Not just a hastily conscripted recruit, but a member of the gang.

As he climbed in, Latham tried to picture that: All police, all taxi drivers, broadcasting companies, telephone firms— what was it Codred had said: ". . . Let you thresh around in the net for a few hours."

The Taxi-Air was moving. Latham sat stiffly, watching it twist up and up the inclined plane. Abruptly, they were out on the runway, speeding. The throbbing of the rocket tubes was loud for an instant, as the mufflers were partially opened. Then they were closed down; and there was only a faint purr of power. Latham glanced into the forward viewers. In the far distance straight ahead loomed the fifteen-story Many Nations Hospital. Five minutes, he estimated, at city speeds.

Five minutes; Latham shook with a sudden appalled consciousness of what he had done. He had climbed into this Taxi-Air knowing what the driver was. He could attack, of course, physically. Except that the driver looked too big, *was* too big, too alert, and in good condition. These psychomedicians, Latham thought in agony. Why hadn't he ever taken exercise? With an automatic will to find some blunt instrument, he poked into the side pockets of the machine. They were empty. A quick glance into the viewers showed—

Three minutes to go!

As the swift seconds passed he began to brace himself. For there was nothing for it but an attack. He could already see himself being smashed by fists, his head crunched against the dashboard by hamlike muscles, his eyes blackened. He had attended assault and battery victims; and he had the thought that it was to his credit that he didn't let the remembrance slow his gathering will to desperate action.

But if only he had some instrument, something heavier than his fists. His gaze lighted on Miss Segill's tightly clutched purse. "What's in there?" Latham hissed in a spurt of hope. "Anything heavy, solid?"

He had the wild feeling that his *sotto voce* was so loud that the driver must hear. But a glance at the rear-view mirror showed that the part of the man's face visible in it was calm. It was an honest countenance, a little tense, but untroubled by recent disturbance. It was impossible to let himself think of the meaning of the unmistakable honesty that reflected in every ripple of the fellow's expression.

Miss Segill said, "There's nothing in the purse. My notebook, odds and ends. What's the matter? Is anything wrong? I've been intending to ask about the phone—"

She didn't suspect. Actually, of course, only a man with his training could know the truth. Latham cut her off by snatching the bag from her fingers. There was the notebook, two change purses, a mirror, a host of metal containers of rouge, lipstick, and other toilet accessories. But the metal was the noncombustible magnesium alloy, slangily called Maggie's Dream by the light metal trades, but something far swankier in the cosmetics field—Latham couldn't remember what. It didn't matter. There wasn't a thing in the bag that weighed over four ounces. The whole purse, including the cunningly shaped hardwood clasps, including the hundred separate items inside, wouldn't run to much over five pounds.

His mind paused, Five pounds? He saw that the plane was sinking down. There was a great, shining roof below—not a moment to ponder the anaesthetic value of five pounds of fluff. He clutched the bag, clasp downward. He leaped forward. He struck. And struck again and again. And again and again and again. Somewhere deep in his brain was startled recognition that fear was making him merciless.

The driver's head sagged, then his body crumpled. Latham stared dully down at the unconscious body. Without a word, finally, he handed Miss Segill her purse. With only a glance at her dazed face, he set himself to the task of dragging the driver into the rear section. He couldn't do it. He felt like a rag, his muscles lifeless. The heavy body came so far, then wouldn't budge.

In the viewer, Latham saw that the hospital's shining roof was behind them now, receding slowly. He leaned over the driver and pulled the hand accelerator hard over. The machine picked up speed. The jar of acceleration was too much for him. Exhausted, Latham collapsed into the seat beside Miss Segill. He sat there dully for a moment, but swiftly his spirits lifted. Safe! They need only get rid of the driver, then roar on eastward at top speed.

"He's coming to!" Miss Segill whispered.

"Give me your purse!" said Latham. "And then give me a hand with him."

A minute later they had the bulky carcass in the rear compartment. Latham climbed over to the front and pulled a parachute out of the emergency locker. As he dumped the driver overboard, he pulled the cord. He watched the chute open up like a great white umbrella with a human pendulum swinging below it. The spectacle intrigued him for a moment, but then he remembered where he was. He slid into the driver's seat, and pressed down on the highly sensitive foot accelerator.

He turned to smile at Miss Segill. His smile faded. The young woman was staring fixedly into the rear-view mirror. She must have caught his glance from the corner of her eyes. She faced him jerkily.

"There're some air blasts behind us," she gulped. "They look like police or something. Do you think—"

It didn't, Latham reflected bitterly, need any thought.

He was conscious of a sense of resignation as he studied the air blasts. There were seven of them. All were long and black, with the very stubby wings of the extremely fast, ultra-modern police patrol craft. Even yet it was hard to believe that they were really police. With abrupt decision, Latham flicked on the short-range radio, about which cynical drivers had often said: "I'd rather lean out and yell!"

Latham smiled grimly at the recollection, then said into the mouthpiece, "What do you want?"

A young man's face formed on the dashboard screen.

"You!" he said.

"Do you realize that I am an agent of Congress, acting for the President of the United States?"

The answer came coolly. "We don't recognize either Congress or the President. You'd better surrender."

Latham was silent. He felt the shock gathering into him again. The young man looked American. His voice, his accent sounded so colloquial that the words he spoke seemed but part of a play, one of those impossible dramas along the lines of "It Can't Happen Here!" so popular years before.

An earlier thought came back, stronger now, more dismaying: What did it mean? The shreds of explanation that had been given to him about there being a group of men who consciously thought of themselves as rulers of the world seemed inadequate now. Because Americans wouldn't give allegiance to any group like that. It wasn't a matter for argument. They just wouldn't, that was all. There must be a deadlier explanation, something infinitely threatening.

The stupid thing was that, by capture and—methods—they would find out what he knew, yet killing him wouldn't prevent the CISA from suspecting the hospital. His report, for instance, was due this very night. What did the thirteen rulers hope to gain?

A moment longer Latham stared at that youthful, cool-voiced traitor; then with a gesture broke the connection. He switched the indicator over to "Telephone," dialed the Washington number of the Committee Investigating Subversive Activities that he had tried to contact from the restaurant.

He felt no particular surprise when the face of Codred appeared on the screen. The man said blandly, "What you are confronted with, Dr. Latham, is organization. The radios on all Taxi-Air and air blasts of this city do not connect with the nearest exchange. They connect with our own city's automatic centre. For today only, or rather, so long as you are at large, all calls to Washington will be switched to me and my staff here. We let the harmless ones go through, but will naturally stop you every time. You have been amazingly agile but, of course, you cannot succeed."

"I'm not caught yet," Latham said grimly.

He suppressed the impulse to ask some leading questions, hesitated, then broke the connection. No vital information would be imparted to him at this stage; and it was not the moment to listen to lectures that could have no result except to throw him off guard.

With narrowed eyes, he studied the air blasts. They were quite close now, two of them forging a little ahead of his craft, all pressing nearer. Latham had a sudden mental picture of a newsreel he had seen some years before, in which three police craft were shown catching an air-car. Catching it, grappling on to the standardized grapple rails—to be without which was an offense subject to heavy fine—and swiftly dragging it to the ground.

Theoretically, a driver with his lightning vision should be able to dart rings around pursuers by the mere ability to see faster what was happening around him. Theoretically, that was. Practically, the armored police ships need only cling boldly to their courses, and let him smash his lighter machine against their impregnable hides. Nevertheless, he had the hope. He swung around on Miss Segill.

"Hang on," he shouted. "It's going to be a wild ride. I—"

He stopped, and stared at her. Her face was changing. It was not a subtle transformation. What was missing was the dominating expression of love adoration. If he had been in the back seat with her, he could have frustrated her action. As it was, there was nothing to do but squirm with the beginning of a half-hearted move to climb towards her. She had raised her skirt, exposing a considerable reach of gleaming leg, around which was a holster with a tiny gun in it. *His* gun! She drew the gun and pointed it at Latham.

"I think," she said coolly, "that at this point I can safely do my bit in this business. You will put up your hands, doctor, and keep them up until you're told otherwise."

The plump man at the dinner table made an interrupting gesture with his hands.

"Just a minute, doctor. We've all heard some of the details of this story of course, though the press version was curiously garbled. But this Miss Segill who held you up with your own gun—she's the gorgeous blonde sitting beside you there—your wife?"

Latham said, "Naturally, at that moment I knew what the explanations was for everything. The amazing thing was that I, with my knowledge, shouldn't have guessed earlier. I knew I had not misread Miss . . . eh . . . Segill's feelings for me, nor her character. Just when they got at her it's hard to say, probably the night before. Her instructions must have been to take a hand at a critical moment, and she undoubtedly didn't become aware of those instructions until that moment. Anyway, looking at her there in the Taxi Air, I realized an immensely potent artificial control had been put over her, and what it was."

The plump man said: "The *h* drug."

"The funny thing about that," Latham went on, "is that, like so many potential world-controlling devices of the last century—the submarine, dive bombers, radio X and so on—*h* was invented in the United States. The inventor used it as an aid in the study of the mind, and not one of his students thought of it as a means to world power. I was one of those students, and I know."

"We simply don't go in over here for ideas like that," the other man agreed. "And—"

The hostess cut him off. She had a vague remembrance that the plump man was somebody of importance, but it didn't matter. The greatest inside story of the decade was being told, and told at her table. She was M-A-D-E.

"Go on, doctor!" she said, and her voice was a reptile-like hiss.

Latham was led along the familiar hospital corridor by a dozen men of the patrol craft. He did not look at Miss Segill, except to note once that some of her jaunty confidence was fading, a puzzled look coming into her face.

Codred met them at the door of *the* room. He was smiling gently, but he said nothing, simply stepped aside, and bowed Latham past. The moment he was in, Latham turned, and watched feverishly as Codred admitted Miss Segill and four of the guards. Latham calculated ferociously: Four! That ought to be enough. But they mustn't be allowed to leave the room.

There must have been an intent expression on his face, because Codred shut the door, then said, "They're here just in case you get tough. We abhor scenes but"—he smiled broadly—"we prepare for them. As for Miss Segill"—he faced the girl—"the effect of the *h* drug should be wearing off her any time. So just hand me that gun, please, Miss—thank you." Once more he turned to Latham.

"As you probably know, doctor, the effect of *h* is not permanent. The initial dose must be quite strong, and it must be administered under controlled conditions. Afterwards, a very diluted form will sustain the slave status it sets in the brain. We use the city water system of course. However, no one drinking the diluted form only would be even remotely affected. This is unfortunate in some respects, but to use more would have deadly results on the mass already under control. The necessary rotelike commands are broadcast over the public address system. Is everything clear now?"

It wasn't; not everything. He felt cold and stiff and deadly. The incredible, fantastic, hellish scoundrels using a poison like that so casually and monstrously. With an effort of will Latham pulled himself together. There were a number of things that it was vital to know. And calmness, however titanic the strain of maintaining it, was necessary.

He turned away from Codred, and stared at the dozen men who sat before separate desks along one end of the room. In spite of himself, then, he glanced at the gun. It was mounted between the sixth and seventh desks; and it held him because—he saw with a start—it was not a gun. It was an electrode of very intricate design. It projected from a metal cabinet which rested on a gleamy mobile base. Heavy cables ran from the cabinet into the floor.

Latham groaned softly as he recognized where he had first seen a similar machine. In a big commercial laboratory, a model instrument used by the American inventors for atomic investigations. Very carefully, he walked forward, out of the direct path of the gun, and returned his attention to the rulers of the world.

They had been watching his examination of the electrode with individual degrees of interest varying from indifferent awareness to sharp, curious stares.

More thoughtful now, Latham studied them. He remembered their faces from that first quick glance he had given them at half-past eleven that morning. But certain facts hadn't struck him then. There were not, he saw now, as many Germans as he had believed. Only three. The four others that he had mistaken for Germans were respectively a Pole, an outsized Frenchman, a Spanish Jew, and an Englishman. Of the remaining five men two looked French, one unmistakably English, one Great Russian, and one Greek. Actually, of course, these men were ultra-national, beyond all loyalties to any flag. Codred, he had already decided was an American.

It was the Greek who broke the silence, who said in a deep bass voice, "Enough of this. Inject h into the prisoner. It is important that he make a carefully doctored report to Washington by tonight."

Latham had expected that he was to receive the h drug. But not so quickly. He *had* to have more information first. He opened his mouth to say something, anything, that would give him some, at least, of the facts he craved. Before he could speak, Codred's voice came resonantly from behind him:

"Not so fast, Michael, not so fast. A man who receives h knowing what it is must have his mind reduced to a condition where it feels helpless against the forces that are attacking it. We have shown Dr. Latham that he cannot escape us. Literally cannot. This will have had a profoundly disconcerting effect. But we must not forget that we are dealing with a psychomedician. Therefore—"

His voice paused tantalizingly. He came around from behind Latham, smiling sardonically. "Let me explain, doctor," he purred, "just what you are up against. We're a very old organization, *very* old. Our leader group, which you see before you, can trace itself back to the year 3417 B.C.. When a member dies, the survivors after careful consideration, elect a replacement. With such extraordinary insight has this been done that our existence has only been suspected occasionally, never actually believed in. In the last six hundred years, no less than twelve kings have held office on our board of rulers. Until recently, no war was fought in Europe that did not have our sanction. Napoleon was a usurper, but he didn't last long; even England helped to down him.

"For many generations now, it has been our intention to bring England under our control. England is our great mistake. We dismissed her from our early calculations, completely underestimating her possibilities. All our troubles have originated from that basic error of judgment. As a direct result of England's independence, America came into being, and, more indirectly—though I could trace every step for you beyond question were I so minded—Soviet Russia. England alone, of course, would in recent generations have been helpless. Twice now, America has thwarted our will to bring England into line. It became apparent that we must first and finally neutralize the United States.

"We came to America under great difficulties. That incredible immigration law had to be got round by means of this hospital. Through the hospital, we slowly built up our control over this one city. It has been an exhausting process, but now we are ready. Starting today, we expand. When you return to Washington, it will be as our enslaved agent. We anticipate that you will be able to make the highest contacts, and will inject h into hundreds of key administration minds. America will not again interfere with our plans. Now"—his voice, which had risen to a harsh pitch, quieted—"have you anything to say while you are still able to think for yourself?"

It was a hard question to answer immediately. Hard because rage was back, choking, clogging his throat. The cold-blooded account of an organization that from time immemorial, had used entire peoples as pawns in an involved play for power, whose members felt no twinge of conscience at the thought of enslavement of hundreds of millions— words could not but be inadequate. Besides, the important thing for him was: Had Codred been telling the truth?

With a remorseless precision, Latham went over in his mind the shifting design of expression that had marked Codred's face as he talked. It had fooled him before, when the man was acting as his guide, and he mustn't let it do so again.

What counted in reading a mind, from the subtle variations of the natural physical reactions, was to miss no response of a vital organ. The older a person, the easier, because blood vessels came to the surface of the nose, the cheeks, and the body generally. The blood-stream was overwhelmingly the most expressive. Muscles rippled under more or less rigid conditions, but blood was a fluid, capable of a thousand subtle transformations. A score of glands pumped their juices into it to balance every emotion, every thought. Veins contracted, arteries swelled, obscure blood vessels dilated and changed color, always for a reason. The man who could connect cause and effect, as he could, could almost literally read thoughts.

And there was no doubt. Codred had not lied. The facts were as stated.

One thing more: He had to know which desk controlled the electrode. He could not permit it to be discharged. So long as it was *live*, he was vulnerable.

Latham began, "Yes, I have a few words to say; words that will puzzle you at first because they involve discussion of the different approaches to the same subject, of two types of mind. You are the ruler type. Your interest in a drug like h has, I venture to say, never extended beyond a careful examination of its utility in serving your ends. But the drug h is merely a positive form of hypnosis. It affects the same region of the brain.

"You would be amazed how many things the late, great Dr. Nanning and his students, of whom I had the honor to be one, discovered about hypnosis and control of the mind through the use of the h drug. I say "amazed" deliberately, because I feel confident that none of you has felt the slightest interest in the purely scientific aspects of h. Do you know, for instance, that hypnotism is nothing less than control of a second personality, and that this extra being is always consciously aware of the first, though the reverse is not true? When you inject h, you release the second personality, and because of its slavelike attributes, are able to control it.

"What will astound you is that, not only does every human body contain the two personalities, that is, the conscious and the second, but also a third. This was discovered by the early French mesmerists, notably Coué, though only h makes control of this third personality easy. When I tell you that this third personality is aware of, and can supersede, *both* of the other two, you will—"

They had been startlingly slow to grasp their doom. Perhaps it was hard for men of their historical background to comprehend even the idea of a final ending to their tremendous and ruthless activities. But once they did understand, they acted.

The alertly watching Latham saw the facial transformations that showed where the electrode controls were. "The sixth and seventh desks!" he shouted. "FIRE!"

The guns of the four guards went off as one shot.

After a minute of silence, the plump man said:

"I recognize that my argument, foreseeing the triumph of the artificial over the natural, has been defeated. Your understanding and control of the *natural* functions of the human mind made your great victory possible. I suppose you evoked the third personalities of the guards while they were escorting you from the ship?"

Latham nodded; then, "Don't give up your argument too quickly. Don't forget that I could not have accomplished what I did except for the fact that the guards were under *h* influence."

The plump man responded with finality: "I accept defeat."

dear pen pal

DEAR PEN PAL:

When I first received your letter from the interstellar correspondence club, my impulse was to ignore it. The mood of one who has spent the last seventy planetary periods—years I suppose you would call them—in an Aurigaen prison, does not make for a pleasant exchange of letters. However, life is very boring, and so I finally settled myself to the task of writing you.

Your description of Earth sounds exciting. I would like to live there for a while, and I have a suggestion in this connection, but I won't mention it till I have developed it further.

You will have noticed the material on which this letter is written. It is a highly sensitive metal, very thin, very flexible, and I have enclosed several sheets of it for your use. Tungsten dipped in any strong acid makes an excellent mark on it. It is important to me that you do write on it, as my fingers are too hot—literally—to hold your paper without damaging it.

I'll say no more just now. It is possible you will not care to correspond with a convicted criminal, and therefore I shall leave the next move up to you. Thank you for your letter. Though you did not know its destination, it brought a moment of cheer into my drab life.

SKANDER.
Aurigae II

DEAR PEN PAL:

Your prompt reply to my letter made me happy. I am sorry your doctor thought it excited you too much, and sorry, also, if I have described my predicament in such a way as to make you feel badly. I welcome your many questions, and I shall try to answer them all.

You say the international correspondence club has no record of having sent any letters to Aurigae. That, according to them, the temperature on the second planet of the Aurigae sun is more than 500 degrees Fahrenheit. And that life is not known to exist there. Your club is right about the temperature and the letters. We have what your people would call a hot climate, but then we are not a hydrocarbon form of life, and find 500 degrees very pleasant.

I must apologize for deceiving you about the way your first letter was sent to me. I didn't want to frighten you away by telling you too much at once. After all, I could not be expected to know that you would be enthusiastic to hear from me.

The truth is that I am a scientist, and, along with the other members of my race, I have known for some centuries that there were other inhabited systems in the galaxy. Since I am allowed to experiment in my spare hours, I amused myself in attempts at communication. I have developed several simple systems for breaking in on galactic communication operations, but it was not until I developed a subspacewave control that I was able to draw your letter (along with several others, which I did not answer) into a cold chamber.

I use the cold chamber as both sending and receiving centre, and since you were kind enough to use the material which I sent you, it was easy for me to locate your second letter among the mass of mail that accumulated at the nearest headquarters of the interstellar correspondence club.

How did I learn your language? After all, it is a simple one, particularly the written language seems easy. I had no difficulty with it. If you are still interested in writing me, I shall be happy to continue the correspondence.

SKANDER.

Aurigae II

DEAR PEN PAL:

Your enthusiasm is refreshing. You say that I failed to answer your questions about how I expected to visit Earth. I confess I deliberately ignored the question, as my experiment had not yet proceeded far enough. I want you to bear with me a short time longer, and then I will be able to give you the details. You are right in saying that it would be difficult for a being who lives at a temperature of 500 degrees Fahrenheit to mingle freely with the people of Earth. This was never my intention, so please relieve your mind. However, let us drop that subject for the time being.

I appreciate the delicate way in which you approach the subject of my imprisonment. But it is quite unnecessary. I performed forbidden experiments upon my body in a way that was deemed to be dangerous to the public welfare. For instance, among other things, I once lowered my surface temperature to 150 degrees Fahrenheit, and so shortened the radio-active cycle-time of my surroundings. This caused an unexpected break in the normal person to person energy flow in the city where I lived, and so charges were laid against me. I have thirty more years to serve. It would be pleasant to leave my body behind and tour the universe—but as I said I'll discuss that later.

I wouldn't say that we're a superior race. We have certain qualities which apparently your people do not have. We live longer, not because of any discoveries we've made about ourselves, but because our bodies are built of a more enduring element—I don't know your name for it, but the atomic weight is 52.9??.* Our scientific discoveries are of the kind that would normally be made by a race with our kind of physical structure. The fact that we can work with temperatures of as high as—I don't know just how to put that—has been very helpful in the development of the subspace energies which are extremely hot, and require delicate adjustments. In the later stages these adjustments can be made by machinery, but in the development the work must be done by "hand"—I put the word in quotes, because we have no hands in the same way that you have.

I am enclosing a photographic plate, properly cooled and chemicalized for your climate. I wonder if you would set it up and take a picture of yourself. All you have to do is arrange it properly on the basis of the laws of light—that is, light travels in straight lines, so stand in front of it—and when you are ready *think* "Ready!" The picture will be automatically taken.

Would you do this for me? If you are interested, I will also send you a picture of myself, though I must warn you. My appearance will probably shock you.

Sincerely,
SKANDER.

*A radioactive isotope of chromium.—Author's Note.

Planet Aurigae II

DEAR PEN PAL:
Just a brief note in answer to your question. It is not necessary to put the plate into a camera. You describe this as a dark box. The plate will take the picture when you think, "Ready!" I assure you it will be flooded with light.

SKANDER.

Aurigae II

DEAR PEN PAL:
You say that while you were waiting for the answer to my last letter you showed the photographic plate to one of the doctors at the hospital—I cannot picture what you mean by doctor or hospital, but let that pass—and he took the problem up with government authorities. Problem? I don't understand. I thought we were having a pleasant correspondence, private and personal.

I shall certainly appreciate your sending that picture of yourself.

SKANDER.

Aurigae II

DEAR PEN PAL:
I assure you I am not annoyed at your action. It merely puzzled me, and I am sorry the plate has not been returned to you. Knowing what governments are, I can imagine that it will not be returned to you for some time, so I am taking the liberty of enclosing another plate.

I cannot imagine why you should have been warned against continuing this correspondence. What do they expect me to do?—eat you up at long distance? I'm sorry but I don't like hydrogen in my diet.

In any event, I would like your picture as a memento of our friendship, and I will send mine as soon as I have received yours. You may keep it or throw it away, or give it to your governmental authorities—but at least I will have the knowledge that I've given a fair exchange.

With all best wishes,

SKANDER.

Aurigae II

DEAR PEN PAL:

Your last letter was so slow in coming that I thought you had decided to break off the correspondence. I was sorry to notice that you failed to enclose the photograph, puzzled by your reference to having a relapse, and cheered by your statement that you would send it along as soon as you felt better—whatever that means. However, the important thing is that you did write, and I respect the philosophy of your club which asks its members not to write of pessimistic matters. We all have our own problems which we regard as overshadowing the problems of others. Here I am in prison, doomed to spend the next 30 years tucked away from the main stream of life. Even the thought is hard on my restless spirit, though I know I have a long life ahead of me after my release.

In spite of your friendly letter, I won't feel that you have completely re-established contact with me until you send the photograph.

Yours in expectation,
SKANDER.

Aurigae II

DEAR PEN PAL:

The photograph arrived. As you suggest, your appearance startled me. From your description I thought I had mentally reconstructed your body. It just goes to show that words cannot really describe an object which has never been seen.

You'll notice that I've enclosed a photograph of myself, as I promised I would. Chunky, Metallic-looking chap, am I not, very different, I'll wager, than you expected? The various races with whom we have communicated become wary of us when they discover we are highly radio-active, and that literally we are a radio-active form of life, the only such (that we know of) in the universe. It's been very trying to be so isolated and, as you know, I have occasionally mentioned that I had hopes of escaping not only the deadly imprisonment to which I am being subjected but also the body which cannot escape.

Perhaps you'll be interested in hearing how far this idea has developed. The problem involved is one of exchange of personalities with someone else. Actually, it is not really an exchange in the accepted meaning of the word. It is necessary to get an impression of both individuals, of their mind and of their thoughts as well as their bodies. Since this phase is purely mechanical, it is simply a matter of taking complete photographs and of exchanging them. By complete I mean of course every vibration must be registered. The next step is to make sure the two photographs are exchanged, that is, that each party has somewhere near him a complete photograph of the other. (It is already too late, Pen Pal. I have set in motion the subspace energy interflow between the two plates, so you might as well read on). As I have said it is not exactly an exchange of personalities. The original personality in each individual is suppressed, literally pushed back out of the consciousness, and the image personality from the "photographic" plate replaces it.

You will take with you a complete memory of your life on Earth, and I will take along memory of my life on Aurigae. Simultaneously, the memory of the receiving body will be blurrily at our disposal. A part of us will always be pushing up, striving to regain consciousness, but always lacking the strength to succeed.

As soon as I grow tired of Earth, I will exchange bodies in the same way with a member of some other race. Thirty years hence, I will be happy to reclaim my body, and you can then have whatever body I last happened to occupy.

This should be a very happy arrangment for us both. You, with your short life expectancy, will have outlived all your contemporaries and will have had an interesting experience. I admit I expect to have the better of the exchange—but now, enough of explanation. By the time you reach this part of the letter it will be me reading it, not you. But if any part of you is still aware, so long for now, Pen Pal. It's been nice having all those letters from you. I shall write you from time to time to let you know how things are going with my tour.

SKANDER.

Aurigae II

DEAR PEN PAL:

Thanks a lot for forcing the issue. For a long time I hesitated about letting you play such a trick on yourself. You see, the government scientists analyzed the nature of that first photographic plate you sent me, and so the final decision was really up to me. I decided that anyone as eager as you were to put one over should be allowed to succeed.

Now I know I don't have to feel sorry for you. Your plan to conquer Earth wouldn't have got anywhere, but the fact that you had the idea ends the need for sympathy.

By this time you will have realized for yourself that a man who has been paralyzed since birth, and is subject to heart attacks, cannot expect a long life span. I am happy to tell you that your once lonely pen pal is enjoying himself, and I am happy to sign myself with a name to which I expect to become accustomed.

With best wishes,
SKANDER.

the sound

"YOU'RE wanted on the video," said Exchange.

Craig clicked on his machine. "Yes?" he said, before the picture could form.

"It's me George." The woman whose face grew on to the videoplate looked agitated. "George, the Play Square just called me. Diddy has gone out to look for the sound."

"Oh," said George.

He studied her image. Hers was normally a good-looking face, clear-skinned, well-shaped, crowned with beautifully coiled black hair. At the moment it was not normal. Her eyes were widened, her muscles tensed, and her hair slightly displaced.

"Veda," he said sharply, "you're not letting it get you."

"But he's out there. And the whole area is said to be full of Yevd spies." She shuddered as she spoke the name of the great enemy.

"The Play Square let him go, didn't it? It must think he's ready."

"But he'll be out all night."

Craig nodded slowly. "Look, darling, this had to happen. It's part of growing up, and we've been expecting it since his ninth birthday last May."

He broke off. "How about you going and doing some shopping? That'll take your mind off him for the rest of the afternoon anyway. Spend"—he made a quick calculation, took another look at her face, and revised the initial figure upward—"five hundred dollars. On yourself. Now, good-bye; and don't worry."

He broke the connection hastily, and climbed to his feet. For a long time he stood at the window staring down at The Yards. From his vantage point he could not see the "Way" or the ship; they were on the other side of the building. But the fairyland of streets and buildings that he could see enthralled him now as always. The Yards were a suburb of Solar City, and that massive metropolis in its artificial tropical setting was a vision that had no parallel in the human-controlled part of the Galaxy. Its buildings and its parks extended to every hazy horizon.

He drew his gaze back from the distance, back to the city proper of The Yards. Slowly, he turned from the window. Somewhere down there his nine-year-old son was exploring the world of sound. Thinking about that or about the Yevd wouldn't do either Veda or himself the slightest good.

He picked up the microfilm of a ninety-foot square blueprint, slipped it into a projector, and began to study it.

By the time the sky grew dark, Diddy knew that the sound never ended. After wondering about it for his whole lifetime, or so it seemed, that was good to know. He'd been told that it ended somewhere out there—vaguely. But this afternoon he'd proved for himself that, no matter how far you went, the sound remained.

The fact that his elders had lied to him about that did not disturb Diddy. According to his robot teacher, the Play Square, parents sometimes fibbed to test a fellow's ingenuity and self-reliance. This was obviously one of the fibs, which he had now disproved.

For all these years, the sound had been in his Play Square, and in the living-room whether he was silent or trying to talk, and in the dining-room making a rhythm out of the eating noises of Mum and Dad and himself—on those days that he was permitted to eat with them. At night the sound crept into bed with him, and while he slept, even in his deepest sleep, he could feel it throbbing in his brain.

Yes, it was a familiar thing, and it was natural that he'd tried to find out if it stopped at the end of first one street and then another. Just how many streets he'd turned up and into and along, whether he'd gone east or west or south or north, was no longer clear. But wherever he'd gone, the sound had followed him. He'd had dinner an hour before at a little restaurant. Now it was time to find out where the *sound* began.

Diddy paused to frown over his location. The important thing was to figure out just where he was in relation to The Yards. He was figuring it by mentally calculating the number of streets between Fifth and Nineteenth, H and R, Centre and Right, when he happened to glance up. There, a hundred feet away was a man he'd first seen three blocks and ten minutes back.

Something about the movement of the man stirred a curious unpleasant memory, and for the first time he saw how dark the sky had become.

He began to walk casually across the road, and he was glad to notice that he was not afraid. His hope was that he would be able to get by the man, and so back to the more crowded Sixth Street. He hoped, also, that he was mistaken in his recognition of the man as Yevd.

His heart sank as a second man joined the first, and the two started to cross the street to intercept him. Diddy fought an impulse to turn and run. Fought it, because if they were Yevd, they could move ten times as fast as a grown man. Their appearance of having a human-like body was an illusion which they could create by their control of light. It was that that had made him suspect the first of the two. In turning the corner, the fellow's legs had walked *wrong*. Diddy could not remember how many times the Play Square had described such a possibility of wrongness, but now he had seen it, he realized that it was unmistakable. In the daytime, the Yevd were said to be more careful with their illusions. Just for a moment, being virtually alone on a dark corner, the Yevd had allowed the human image to blur.

"Boy!"

Diddy slowed, and looked around at the two men, as if seeing them for the first time.

"Boy, you're out on the streets rather late."

"This is my exploring night, sir," said Diddy.

The "man" who had spoken reached into his breast pocket. It was a curious gesture, not complete, as if in creating the illusion of the movement, he hadn't quite thought through the intricacies of such an action. Or perhaps he was careless in the gathering darkness. His hand came out, and flashed a badge.

"We're 'Yard' agents," he said. "We'll take you to the 'Way'."

He put the badge back into his pocket, or seemed to, and motioned towards the brightness in the distance. Diddy knew better than to resist.

Out of the dark distance of space the Yevd had come more than two hundred years before. Like the black reaches through which their ships plunged from their multitudinous worlds in the central mass of the Galaxy, they made an uneasy impression on the minds of men.

In the beginning, they did not try to look human, and there was no suspicion that they could control light and related energies with their bodies. Then one day, accidentally, a "man" was blasted while rifling the vault of the Research Council. Dead, the man-image faded, and there, sprawled on the marble floor was the dark, rectangular, elongated shape with its score of reticulated, piston-like arms and legs.

On that day, more than two centuries before, a dismayed government acted swiftly and secretly. The fleet was mobilized while the ramifications of the plot were explored. Armed helicars flew along the streets of every city. The probing beams of radar machines reflected and silhouetted the real bodies of the Yevd—though it was afterwards discovered that the radar method was successful only because of the element of surprise. The Yevd had become careless because they were not suspected, and maintained their illusion only on the light level visible to human beings. Because of that error, nearly a million of them were blasted on Earth alone, and that broke the fifth column there.

Warnings had meanwhile been flashed to all the man-inhabited planets. There, also, prompt action averted disaster. Altogether thirty-seven million Yevd were killed.

Thereafter, Earth and Yevd ships fought each other on sight. The intensity of the war waxed and waned. There were several agreements, but at no time did these actually stop the war. To some extent they stopped Yevd ships from coming into man-controlled space and *vice versa*. The most recent agreement included an exchange of ambassadors, but five years before a Yevd colonizing expedition had occupied a star system ninety-odd light-years nearer Earth than any other sun in their galactic empire. When asked to explain the seizure, the Yevd ambassador had stated that the "action is a normal incident in the expansion of a great power, and is not directed at anyone." He was promptly handed his papers, and six months later the sound began.

The Yevd were a hydrocarbon-flourine-oxygen life form, tough of muscle and skin, physically stronger than man, immune to ordinary poisons and corrosives. Their control of light gave them an additional advantage; and the combination of enormous capability of unceasing aggressiveness had finally decided the United Governments to make a major counter-attack.

The big ship was designed to do the job.

Craig opened the door of his apartment for the two police officers shortly after dinner. Though they wore plain clothes, he recognized them instantly for what they were.

"Mr. Craig?" one of them asked.

"Yes?"

"George Craig?"

He nodded this time, aware, in spite of having just eaten, of an empty sensation.

"You are the father of Diryl Dexter Craig, aged nine?"

Craig took hold of the door jamb. "Yes ," he mumbled.

The spokesman said: "It is our duty, as required by law, to inform you that at this moment your son is in the control of two Yevd, and that he will be in grave danger of his life for some hours to come."

Craig said: "I'm . . . not . . . sure . . . I understand."

Quietly, the officer described how Diddy had been taken over on the sidewalk. He added, "We've been aware for some time that the Yevd have been concentrating in Solar City in more than usual numbers. Naturally, we haven't located them. As you may know, we estimate their numbers on the basis of those we do spot."

Craig hadn't known, but he said nothing.

The other continued: "As you probably also know, we are more interested in discovering the purpose of a Yevd ring than in capturing individuals. As with all Yevd schemes in the past, this one will probably prove to be extremely devious. It seems clear that we have only witnessed the first step of an intricate plan. But now, are there any questions?"

Craig hesitated. He was acutely conscious of Veda in the kitchen putting the dinner dishes into the dish washing machine. It was vital that he get these policemen away before she found out what their mission was. Yet one question he had to ask.

"You mean, there'll be no immediate attempts to rescue Diddy?"

The officer said in a firm voice: "Until we have the information we want, this situation will be allowed to ripen. I have been instructed to ask you not to build up any hopes.

As you know, a Yevd can actually concentrate energy of blaster power with his cells. Under such circumstances, death can strike very easily."

He broke off, "That's all, sir. You may call from time to time if you desire further information. The police will not communicate with you again on their own initiative."

"Thank you," said Craig automatically.

He closed the door, and went with mechanical stolidity back to the living-room. Veda called from the kitchen:

"Who was it, darling?"

Craig drew a deep breath. "Somebody looking for a man named George Craig. They got the right name but the wrong man." His voice held steady for the words.

"Oh!" said Veda.

She must have forgotten the incident at once, for she did not mention it again. Craig went to bed at ten o'clock. He lay there, conscious of a vague ache in his back, and a sick feeling at the pit of his stomach. At one o'clock he was still wide awake.

He mustn't offer any resistance. He must make no attempt to frustrate any plans they might have. For years the Play Square had emphasized that. No young person, it had stated categorically, should consider himself qualified to judge how dangerous any particular Yevd might be, Or how important the plan of a Yevd spy ring.

Assume that something was being done. And await whispered instructions.

Diddy was remembering all these things, as he walked between the two Yevd, his short legs twinkling as he was hustled along faster than his normal pace. He was heartened by the fact that they had still not let him know their identity. They were still pretending.

The street grew tremendously brighter. Ahead, he could see the ship silhouetted against the blue-black sky beyond. All the buildings that crowded the "Way" were giving off the sunlight they'd absorbed during the day. The hundred story administration building glowed like a jewel in the shadow of the towering ship, and all the other buildings shone with an intensity of light that varied according to their sizes.

With Diddy in tow, the two Yevd came to Cross 2. The "Way" itself was Cross 1.

They walked across the street, and came to the barrier. The two Yevd paused in front of the eight-foot-wide band of fluted metal, with its constant suction effect, and stared down at the open ventilators.

Two centuries before, when Yevd and human first made contact, there had been concrete walls or electrified barbed wire fences around defense plants and military areas. Then it was discovered that Yevd could deflect electric current, and that their tough skin was impervious to the sharp bite of barbed wire. Concrete was equally ineffective. The walls had a habit of crumbling in the presence of certain Yevd-directed energies. And among workmen who arrived to repair them was usually a Yevd who, by a process of image transference and murder, made his way inside. Armed patrols were all too frequently killed to a man, and their places taken by Yevd light-wave images.

The air suction type of barrier was only a few generations old. It extended all the way around The Yards. Human beings who walked through it scarcely noticed it. A Yevd who tried to penetrate it died within about three minutes.

It was one of Man's top secrets.

Diddy seized on the hesitation of his two escorts. "Thanks for bringing me this far," he said, "I'll be able to manage now."

One of the "men" laughed. It was wonderfully authentic laughter, considering that it came from a sound box embedded in the Yevd's shoulder muscles.

The creature said: "You know kid, you look like a pretty good sport. Just to show you that our hearts are in the right places, how'd you like to have a little fun—just for a minute?"

"Fun?" said Diddy.

"See that barrier there?"

Diddy nodded.

"Good. As we've already told you, we're security police— you know, anti-Yevd. Of course, we've got the problem on our minds all the time. You can see that, can't you?"

Diddy said that he could. He wondered what was coming.

"Well, the other day my friend and I were talking about our job, and we figured out a way by which a Yevd might be able to cross that barrier. It seemed so silly that we thought we ought to test it before we reported it to the top brass. You know what I mean. If it turned out wrong, why, we'd look foolish. That's the test we want you to help us make."

No young person ... must ... attempt to frustrate any plans ... of a Yevd spy ring. The command, so often given by the Play Square, echoed in Diddy's mind. It seemed dreadfully clear that here was special danger, and yet it was not for him to judge, or oppose. The years of training made that automatic now. He wasn't old enough to know.

"All you've got to do," said the Yevd spokesman, "is walk between those two lines across the barrier, and then walk back again."

The lines indicated were a part of the pattern of the fluted arrangement of the ventilators. Without a word of objection, Diddy walked across to the other side. Just for a moment then, he hesitated, half minded to make a run for it to the safety of a building thirty feet away. He changed his mind. They could blast him before he could go ten feet.

Dutifully, he came back, as he had been told to do.

A score of men were coming along the street. As they came near, Diddy and the two Yevd drew aside to let them pass. Diddy watched them hopefully. Police? he wondered. He wanted desperately to be sure that all that was happening was suspected.

The workmen trooped by, walked noisily across the barrier, and disappeared behind the nearest building.

"This way, kid," said the Yevd. "We've got to be careful that we're not seen."

Diddy wasn't so sure of that, but he followed them reluctantly into the dark space between two buildings.

"Hold out your hand."

He held it out, tense and scared. *I'm going to die*, he thought. And he had to fight back the tears. But his training won out, and he stood still as a needle-sharp pain jabbed his finger.

"Just taking a sample of your blood, kid. You see, the way we look at it, that suction system out there conceals high-powered air hypodermics, which send up bacteria to which the Yevd are vulnerable. Naturally, these air hypodermics send up their shots of bacteria at about a thousand miles an hour, so fast that they penetrate your skin without you feeling them or leaving a mark. And the reason the suction ventilators keep pulling in so much air is to prevent the bacteria from escaping into the atmosphere. And also the same culture of bacteria is probably used over and over again. You see where that leads us?"

Diddy didn't, but he was shocked to the core of his being. For this analysis sounded right. It *could* be bacteria that were being used against the Yevd. It was said that only a few men knew the nature of the defense projected by the innocent-looking barrier. Was it possible that at long last the Yevd were finding it out?

He could see that the second Yevd was doing something in the shadowy region deeper between the two buildings. There were little flashes of light. Diddy made a wild guess, and thought: *He's examining my blood with a microscope to see how many dead anti-Yevd bacteria are in it.*

The Yevd who had done all the talking so far said: "You see how it is kid, you can walk across that barrier, and the bacteria that are squirted up from it die immediately in your bloodstream. Our idea is this: There can only be one type of bacteria being sent up in any one area. Why? Because, when they're sucked down, and sent back to the filter chambers so they can be removed from the air and used again, it would be too complicated if there were more than one type of bacteria. The highly virulent bacteria that thrive in a fluorine compound are almost as deadly to each other as to the organism which they attack. It's only when one type is present in enormously predominant amounts that it is so dangerous to the Yevd. In other words, only one type at a time can kill a Yevd.

"Obviously, if a Yevd is shot full of immunization against that particular type of bacteria—why, kid, he can cross the barrier *at that point* as easily as you can, and he can then do anything he wants to inside The Yards. You see how big a thing we're working on."

He broke off, "Ah, I see my friend has finished examining your blood. Wait here a moment."

He moved off to where the other Yevd was waiting. There were tiny flashes of light from the darkness, and Diddy remembered tensely that Yevd communicated with each other by light beams and light energies that operated directly from a complex interrelation of organic prisms, lenses, mirrors, and cell transformers.

The conference, whatever its nature, lasted less than a minute. The Yevd came back.

"O.K., kid, you can scoot along. Thanks a lot for helping us. We won't forget it."

Diddy could not believe his ears for a moment. "You mean, that's all you want from me?" he said.

"That's all."

As he emerged from the dark space between the two buildings, Diddy expected somehow that he would be stopped. But, though the two Yevd followed him out to the street, they made no attempt to accompany him as he started across it toward the barrier.

The spokesman called after him: "There's a couple of other kids coming up the street. You might join them, and the bunch of you can look for the sound together."

Diddy turned to look, and as he did so, two boys came darting towards him, yelling: "Last one over is a pig."

They had the momentum, and they were past him in a flash. As he raced after them, Diddy saw them hesitate, turn slightly, and then cross the barrier at a dead run over the ventilators which he had tested for the two Yevd researchers.

They waited for him on the other side.

"My name is Jackie," said one.

"And mine is Gil," said the second one. He added, "Let's stick together."

Diddy said: "My name is Diddy."

Neither of the two boys seemed to think the name unusual.

There were separate sounds, as the three of them walked, that drowned out *the* sound. Discordant noises. Whirring machines. An intricate pattern of clangorous hammerings. Rippling overtones from the molecular displacement of masses of matter. A rubber-wheeled train hummed towards them over the endless metal floor that carpeted The Yards, and paused as its electronic eyes and ears sensed their presence. They stepped out of the way, and it rushed past. A line of cranes lifted a hundred-ton metal plate on to an antigravity carrier. It floated away lightly, airily, into the blazing sky.

Diddy had never been on the "Way" at night before, and it would have been tremendously exciting if he had not been so miserable. The trouble was, he couldn't be sure. Were these two companions Yevd? So far they had done nothing that ac-

tually proved they were. The fact that they had crossed the
barrier at the point where he had tested it for the two Yevd
could have been a coincidence.

Until he was sure, he dare not tell anyone what had happened. Until he was sure, he would have to go along with
them, and even if they wanted him to do something, co-operate with them. That was the rule. That was the training. He
had a picture in his mind of scores of image-boys crossing the
barrier at the test point. Even now they would be moving
along the "Way," free to do as they pleased.

The universe around the "Way" shivered with a concatena-
tion of sounds. But nowhere that Diddy looked, no doorway
into which he peered, no building that he wandered through
with wide, fascinated eyes—in spite of the presence of his
companions—nowhere was there a sound that did not quickly
fade away as he moved on.

Not once did they come to anything that even faintly
resembled a barrier-type ventilator. If there were any threat
to wandering Yevd, it was not apparent. Doors stood wide
open. He had hoped in a vague fashion that the atmosphere
of some closed room would be deadly for the enemy and not
for him. He found no such rooms.

Worst of all, there was no sign of a human being who
might conceivably protect him from the Yevd, or even suspect their presence. If only he could be sure that these two
boys were Yevd. Or weren't. Suppose they carried some
deadly weapon capable of causing tremendous damage to the
ship?

They came to a building half a mile square. And Diddy
grew suddenly hopeful. His companions offered no objection
as he walked through a huge door on to a causeway. Below
them was depth. From the causeway Diddy looked down at a
dimly glowing world of huge cube-like structures. The top of
the highest cube was at least a quarter of a mile below the
causeway, and it was blocked off by floor after floor of plastic, so limpidly transparent that only a gleam here and there
revealed that there were many layers of hard, frustrating matter protecting the world above from the enormous atomic
piles in that colossal powerhouse.

As he approached the centre of the causeway, Diddy
saw—as he had a few moments before hopefully expected—
that there was somebody in a little transparent structure that

jutted out from the metalwork. A woman, reading. She looked up as the three of them came up, Diddy in the lead.

"Searching for the sound?" she asked in a friendly tone. She added, "Just in case you don't know—I'm a Sensitive."

The other boys were silent. Diddy said that he knew. The Play Square had told him about Sensitives. They could anticipate changes in the flow of an atomic pile. It had, he recalled, something to do with the way the calcium content in their blood was controlled. Sensitives lived to a very old age—around a hundred and eighty—not because of the jobs they had but because they could respond to the calcium rejuvenation processes.

The memory was only a background to his gathering disappointment. Apparently, she had no way of detecting the presence of a Yevd. For she gave no sign.

He'd better keep pretending that he was still interested in the sound, which was true in a way. He said: "Those dynamos down there would make quite a vibration, I guess."

"Yes they would."

Diddy was suddenly intent, impressed but not convinced. "Still, I don't see how it could make the big sound."

She said: "You all seem like nice boys. I'm going to whisper a clue into your ears. You first," she motioned to Diddy.

It seemed odd, but he did not hesitate. She bent down. "Don't be surprised," she whispered. "You'll find a very small gun under the overlapping edge of the metal sidewalk underneath the ship. Go down escalator seven, and turn right. It's just on this side of the beam that has a big H painted on it. Nod your head if you understand."

Diddy nodded.

The woman went on swiftly. "Slip the gun into your pocket. Don't use it until you're ordered to. Good luck."

She straightened. "There," she said, "that should give you an idea."

She motioned to Jackie. "You next."

The stocky boy shook his head. "I don't need no clues," he said. "Besides, I don't want nobody whispering anything to me."

"Nor me either," said Gil.

The woman smiled. "You musn't be shy," she said. "But never mind. I'll give you a clue anyway. Do you know what the word "miasm" means?" She spoke directly to Jackie.

"Mist."

"That's my clue, then, Miasm. And now you'd better be getting along. The sun is due up a few minutes before six, and it's after two o'clock now."

She picked up her book and, when Diddy glanced back a few minutes later, she looked as if she were a part of the chair. She seemed scarcely alive, so still she was. But because of her, he knew. The situation was as deadly as he had suspected. The great ship itself was in danger.

It was towards the ship that he headed.

Craig wakened suddenly to the realization that something had roused him, and that accordingly he must have slept. He groaned inwardly, and started to turn over. If he only *could* sleep through this night.

With a start he grew aware that his wife was sitting on the edge of the bed. He glanced at his illuminated watch. It was 2:22 a.m.

Oh, my gosh, he thought, *I've got to get her back to bed.*

"I can't sleep," said Veda.

Her voice had a whimper in it, and he felt sick. For she was worrying like this about nothing. He pretended to be very thoroughly asleep.

"George."

Craig stirred, but that was all.

"George."

He opened one eye. "Darling, please."

"I wonder how many other boys are out tonight."

George turned over. "Veda, what are you trying to do—keep me awake?"

"Oh, I'm sorry. I didn't mean to." Her tone was not sorry, and after a moment she seemed to have forgotten she'd spoken the words. "George."

He did not answer.

"George, do you think we could find out?"

He'd intended to ignore further conversations, but his mind started to examine the possible meaning of what she'd said. He grew astonished at the meaninglessness of her words, and woke up.

"Find out what?" he said.

"How many there are."

"How many what?"

"Boys—outside tonight."

"Craig who was weighed down by a far more desperate fear, sighed. "Veda, I've got to go to work tomorrow."

"Work!" said Veda, and her voice had an edge in it. "Don't you ever think of anything but work? Haven't you any feelings?" Craig kept his silence, but that was not the way to get her back to her bed. She went on, her voice several tones higher. "The trouble with you men is that you grow callous."

"If you mean by that, am I worried—no, I'm not." That came hard. He thought, *I've got to keep this on the level.* He sat up and turned on the light. He said aloud, "Darling, if it gives you any satisfaction you've succeeded in your purpose. I'm awake."

"It's about time," said Veda. "I think we ought to call up. And if you don't, I will."

Craig climbed to his feet. "O.K., but don't you dare hang over my neck when I'm calling. I refuse to have anybody suspect that I'm a hen-pecked husband. You stay right here."

He found himself relieved that she had forced the issue. He went out of the bedroom and shut the door firmly behind him. On the video, he gave his name. There was a pause, and then a grave-faced man in an admiral's uniform came into view. His image filled the videoplate, as he bent over the videophone in the patrol office.

He said: "Mr. Craig, the situation is as follows: Your son is still in the company of two Yevd. A very ingenious method was used to get across the barrier, and at the present moment we suspect that about a hundred Yevd posing as boys are somewhere in The Yards. Nobody has tried to cross in the last half-hour, so we feel that every Yevd in Solar City who had been prepared in advance against the particular defense we had in that area is now in The Yards. Although they have not yet concentrated on any particular point, we feel that the crisis is imminent."

Craig said in a steady tone: "What about my son?"

"Undoubtedly, they have further plans for him. We are trying to provide him with a weapon, but that would have a limited value at best."

Craig realized wretchedly that they were being very careful to say nothing that would give him any real hope. He said slowly: "You let a hundred of these Yevd get on to the 'Way' without knowing what they are after?" ˌ

The admiral said: "It's important to us to learn their objective. What do they think is worth such a tremendous risk? This is a very courageous enterprise on their part, and it is our duty to let it come to a head. We are reasonably certain of what they are after, but we must be sure. At the final moment, we will make every effort to save your son's life, but we can guarantee nothing."

For a brief moment Craig saw the picture of the affair as these hard men visualized it. To them, Diddy's death would be a regrettable incident, nothing more. The papers would say, "Casualties were light." They might even make a hero out of him for a day.

"I'm afraid," said the admiral, "I'll have to ask you to break off now. At this moment your son is going down under the ship, and I want to give my full attention to him. Goodbye."

Craig broke the connection, and climbed to his feet. He stood for a moment bracing himself, and then he went back into the bedroom. He said cheerfully: "Everything seems to be all right."

There was no reply. He saw that Veda was lying with her head on his pillow. She had evidently lain down to wait his return, and had immediately fallen asleep.

Very carefully he tucked her in, and then crawled into her bed. He was still awake at dawn, restless, tired, and unhappy.

"What'd that dame whisper to you?" asked Jackie.

They were going down the escalator into the tunnel beneath the "Way." Diddy, who had been listening intently for the sound—there wasn't any particular noise—turned.

"Oh, just what she said to you."

Jackie seemed to consider that. They reached the walk and Diddy started immediately along it. Casually, he looked for a metal pillar with an H on it. He saw it abruptly, a hundred feet ahead.

Behind him, Gil spoke: "Why would she go to the trouble of whispering to you, if she was going to tell us anyway?"

Their suspicion made Diddy tremble inside, but his training told. "I think she was just having fun with us kids," he said.

"Fun!" That was Jackie.

Gil said: "What are we doing here under the ship?"

Diddy said: "I'm tired."

He sat down on the edge of the walk beside the five-foot-thick metal beam that reared up into the distance above. He let his feet dangle down to the tunnel proper. The two Yevd walked past him and stood on the other side of the pillar. Diddy thought with a dizzy excitement, *They're going to communicate with each other—or with others.*

He steadied himself, and fumbled under the overlapping edge of the walk with his hand. Swiftly, he ran his fingers along the metal. He touched something. The tiny blaster came easily into his hand, and he slipped it into his pocket in a single synchronized motion. Then, weak from reaction, he sat there.

He grew aware of the vibration of the metal on the bones of his thighs. His special shoes had absorbed most of that tremor, and he had been so intent on the weapon that he hadn't noticed immediately. Now he did. Ever so slightly, his body shook and shivered. He felt himself drawn into the sound. His muscles and organs hummed and quivered. Momentarily, he forgot the Yevd, and for that moment it seemed immeasurably strange to be sitting here on the raw metal, unprotected and in tune with the sound itself.

He'd guessed the vibration would be terrific under the ship of ships. The city of The Yards was built on metal. But all the shock-absorbing material with which the streets and roads were carpeted couldn't muffle the ultimately violent forces and energies that had been concentrated in one small area. Here were atomic piles so hot that they were exploding continuously with a maximum detonation short of cataclysm. Here were machines that could stamp out hundred-ton electro-steel plates.

For eight and a half years more, The Yards would exist on this colossal ship. And then, when it finally flew, he would be on it. Every family in The Yards had been selected for two purposes—because the father or mother had a skill that could be used in the building of the ship, and because they had a child who would grow up in and around the ship.

In no other way, except by growing up with it, would human beings ever learn to understand and operate the spaceship that was rising here like a young mountain. In its ninety-four hundred feet of length was concentrated the engineering genius of centuries, so much specialized knowledge, so much mechanical detail, that visiting dignitaries looked around in bewilderment at the acres of machines and dials and instruments on every floor, and at the flashing wall lights that had already been installed in the lower decks.

He would be on it. Diddy stood up in a shaking excitement of anticipation—just as the two Yevd emerged from behind the pillar.

"Let's go!" said Jackie. "We've fooled around long enough."

Diddy came down from his height of exaltation. "Where to?"

Gil said: "We've been tagging along after you. Now, how about you going where we want to go for a change?"

Diddy did not even think of objecting. "Sure," he said.

The neon sign on the building said "RESEARCH," and there were a lot of boys around. They wandered singly and in groups. He could see others in the distance, looking as if they were going nowhere in particular. It was hard to believe that they were all Yevd, but Diddy had the awful empty feeling that they were.

Research. That was what they were after. Here in this building, human beings had developed the anti-Yevd bacteria of the barrier. Just what the Yevd would want to know about that process, he had no idea. Perhaps, a single bit of information in connection with it would enable them to destroy a source material or organism, and so nullify the entire defense. The Play Square had intimated on occasion that such possibilities existed.

All the doors of "Research" were closed, the first building like that he had seen. Jackie said: "You open up, Diddy."

Obediently, Diddy reached for the door handle. He stopped, as two men came along the walk. One of them hailed him.

"Hello, there kid. We keep running into you, don't we?"

Diddy let go of the door, and turned to face them. They looked like the two "men" who had originally brought him to the barrier, and who had made the bacteria test on him. But that would be merely outward appearance. The only Yevd inside the barrier of all those in Solar City would be individuals who had been immunized against the particular bacteria which he had isolated for them at that one part of the barrier.

It would be too much of a coincidence if both The Yard agent images had belonged to that group. Accordingly, these were not the same.

Not that it mattered.

The spokesman said: "Glad we bumped into you again. We want to conduct another experiment. Now, look, you go inside there. Research is probably protected in a very special fashion. If we can prove our idea here, then we'll have helped in making it harder for the Yevd to come into The Yards. That'll be worth doing, won't it?"

Diddy nodded. He was feeling kind of sick inside, and he wasn't sure he could talk plainly in spite of all his training.

"Go inside," said the Yevd, "stand around for a few moments, and then take a deep breath, hold it in, and come out. That's all."

Diddy opened the door, stepped through into the bright interior. The door closed automatically behind him.

It was a large room in which he found himself. *I could run*, he thought. *They don't dare come in here*. The absence of people inside the room chilled the impulse. It seemed unusual that there was no one around. Most of the departments in The Yards operated on a round-the-clock basis.

Behind him, the door opened. Diddy turned. The only Yevd in sight were Jackie and Gil standing well back from the door, and other boys even further away. Whoever had opened the door was taking no chances on getting a dose of anything, dangerous or otherwise.

"You can come out now," said the man's voice. He spoke from behind the door. "But remember, first take a deep breath and hold it."

Diddy took the breath. The door shut automatically as he emerged. And there were the two Yard "police" waiting behind it. One of them held up a little bottle with a rubber tube. "Exhale into this," he said.

When that was done, the Yevd handed it to his companion who walked quickly around the corner of the building and out of sight.

The spokesman said: "Notice anything unusual?"

Diddy hesitated. The air in the building, now that he thought of it, had seemed thick, a little harder to breathe than ordinary air. He shook his head slowly. "I don't think so," he said.

The Yevd was tolerant. "Well, you probably wouldn't notice, he said. He added quickly, "We might as well test your blood, too. Hold up your finger."

Diddy cringed a little from the needle, but he allowed the blood to be taken. Gil came forward. "Can I help?" he asked eagerly.

"Sure," said the "man." "You take this around to my friend."

Gil was gone as only a boy could go, at a dead run. A minute ticked by, and then another minute; and then—

"Ah," said the "man," "here they come."

Diddy stared at the returning pair with a sickly grin. The Yevd who had been standing beside him, walked swiftly forward to meet the two. If the two "men" said anything to each other, Diddy was unable to hear it. Actually, he took it for granted that there was a swift exchange on the light level.

The communication, whatever its nature, stopped.

The "man" who had done all the talking came back to Diddy, and said: "Kid, you've sure been valuable to us. It looks as if we're really going to make a contribution to the war against the Yevd. Do you know that air in there has an artificial gas mixed with it, a fluorine compound? Very interesting and very safe by itself. And even if a Yevd with his fluorine metabolism should walk in there, he'd be perfectly safe—unless he tried to use the energy of his body on a blaster or communication level. The energy acts as a uniting agent, brings about a chemical union between the fluorine in the air and the fluorine in the Yevd body—and you know what fluorine is like even at room temperatures under the right conditions."

Diddy knew. The chemical reactions of fluorine and its compounds had been a part of his education since the earliest days.

"It flames up violently," said the "man" with apparent satisfaction. "And the Yevd himself is the only one who can set off the explosion. Very clever. But now, I gather that all you kids want to go inside and have a look around. O.K., in with you. Not you"—to Diddy—"not for a minute. I want to have a little talk with you. Come on over here."

He and Diddy drew aside, while the "boys" rushed through the door. Diddy could imagine them spreading through the building, searching out secrets. He thought wearily, *Surely somebody will do something, and quickly.*

The Yevd said: "Confidentially, kid, this is really an important job you've done for us today. Just to give you an idea, we've kept an eye on the Research Building pretty well all night. The staff here usually goes home around midnight. Since midnight, a couple of workmen have gone into the place, installed some equipment, and departed. They put a radio hook-up over the door, with a loud-speaker both inside and out. And that's all that happened. Right now, except for you kids, the whole place is empty. You can see how much the people here have depended on the bacteria barrier keeping the Yevd away."

He paused, then went on, "Of course, the Yevd could spy out most of that information in advance, and if they finally got across the barrier they could set up guards all around the building, and so prevent even the most powerful armored forces from getting through to the defense of the building. It could be blasted, of course, from a distance, and destroyed, but it's hard to imagine them doing that very quickly. They'd wait till they'd tried other methods.

"You see where that would take us. The Yevd would have an opportunity to search out some of the secrets of the building. Once outside, they could communicate the information to other Yevd not in the danger area, and then each individual would have to take his own chance on escaping. That's bold stuff, but the Yevd have done similar things before. So you see, it all could happen easy enough. But now, we've prevented it."

"Diddy"—it was a whisper from above and to one side of him—"don't show any sign that you hear this."

Diddy stiffened, then quickly relaxed. It had been proved long ago that the Yevd electronic hearing and talking devices, located as they were inside sound deadening shoulder muscles, could not detect whispers.

The whispers went on swiftly: "You've got to go inside. When you are inside, stay near the door. That's all. There'll be more instructions for you then."

Diddy located the source of the whisper. It was coming from above the door. He thought shakily: *Those workmen who installed the radio the Yevd mentioned—the whisper must be coming through that.*

But how was he going to get inside when this Yevd was so obviously delaying him?

The Yevd was saying something about a reward, but Diddy scarcely heard. Distractedly, he looked past the "man." He could see a long line of buildings, some of them brightly illuminated, others in a half-darkness. The vast brilliance from the ship cast a long shadow where he was standing. In the sky above, the night seemed as black as ever.

There was no sign of the bright new morning, only hours away now.

Diddy said desperately: "Gosh, I'd better get inside. The sun will soon be up, and I've still got a lot of places to look."

The Yevd said: "I wouldn't waste much time in there. Take a look inside, huh, and tell me what the other kids are doing."

Quivering, Diddy opened the door. And went in. And let the door close behind him in its automatic fashion.

"Diddy," came the whisper, "unless a Yevd carries a weapon right out in the open, then he's dependent on the energy from his cells. A Yevd by his very nature has to wander around without any clothing on. It's only his body that can produce the images of human clothes and human form. Now, think carefully. Did you see any of those boys carrying a weapon? Whisper your answer."

"I don't remember seeing any," said Diddy shakily.

"We'll have to hope that your memory is accurate," came the answer. "If it is, then any weapon they appear to produce will be an image weapon. Now listen, how many boys are in sight?"

There were two, both of them bent over a desk on the other side of the room.

"Two." The whisper echoed his count. "Good. Take out your gun and shoot them."

Diddy put his hand in his pocket, swallowed hard—and brought out the gun. His hand trembled a little, but for five years now he had been trained for such a moment as this, and he felt awfully steady inside. It was not a gun that had to be aimed perfectly.

It fired a steady blue streak of flame, and he merely waved its nozzle towards where the Yevd were. They started to turn. And collapsed as they did so.

"Did you get them?" The whisper again.

"Yes." His voice trembled. Across the room what had been two apple-cheeked boys was changing. In death, the images couldn't hold. And though he had seen pictures of what was emerging, it was different seeing the dark flesh coming into view, the strange legs—

"Listen"—the whisper caught him out of that shock—"all the doors are locked. Nobody can get in, nobody out. Start walking through the building. Shoot everybody you see. *Everybody!* Accept no pleas, no pretence that they are just kids. We've kept track of every other real boy, and there are only Yevd in the building. Burn them all without mercy.

"And, Diddy, I'm sorry this is the way it had to be. But you were the only one we could work through. You were right in there with them. The only reason you're alive is that they probably think you may still be of use to them inside the building, in case something turns up. You are the only one they do not seriously suspect. Any other method we might have used would have cost us hundreds of lives. But now, let's go! You take care of those inside. We'll go after the ones out here.

"And remember your training for caution. Don't go through a doorway until you've looked in. Remember, also, they can't shoot back. If they even try it, their bodies will start on fire. Good luck, Diddy. The battle is all yours."

The trap was so complete that there was not a single moment of real danger to the boy.

It was still pitch dark as Diddy caught a helicar at Cross 2 and flew to within a block of the hill, from which "explorers" like himself had to watch the sun rise. He climbed the steps that led to the top of the hill, and found several other boys already there, sitting and standing around.

While he could not be certain they were human, he had a pretty strong conviction that they were. There seemed to be no reason why a Yevd should participate in this particular ritual.

Diddy sank down under a bush beside the shadow shape of one of the boys. Neither of them spoke right away, then Diddy said: "What's your name?"

"Mart." The answering voice was shrill but not loud.

"Find the sound?" asked Diddy.

"Yep."

"So did I." He hesitated, thinking of what he had done. Just for a moment he had a sharp awareness of how wonderful was the training that had made it possible for a nine-year-old boy to act as he had acted, and then that faded from his fore-consciousness, and he said: "It's been fun, hasn't it?"

"I guess so."

There was silence. From where Diddy sat, he could see the intermittent glare of the atomic furnaces as the sky flared with a white, reflected fire. Further along was the jewel-bright aura of light that partially framed the ship. The sky above was no longer dark, and Diddy noticed that the shadows around him were not dense any more, but grayish. He could see Mart's body crouched under the bush, a smaller body than his own.

As the dawn brightened, he watched the ship. Slowly, the metal of its bare upper ribs caught the flames of the sun that was still not visible from where they sat. The glare expanded downward and sunlight glinted on the dark, shiny vastness of its finished lower walls, the solid shape it made against the sky beyond.

Out of the shadows grew the ship, an unbelievable thing, bigger than anything around it. At this distance the hundred-story Administration Building looked like a part of its scaffolding, a white pillar against the dark colossus that was the ship.

Long after the sun had come up, Diddy stood watching in an exaltation of pride. In the glare of the new day the ship seemed to be gathering itself as if poised for flight. Not yet, Diddy thought shakily, not yet. But the day would come. In that far time the biggest ship ever planned and constructed by men would point its nose at the open spaces between the near stars and fly out in the darkness. And then indeed would the Yevd have to give ground. For they had nothing like this. Nothing even near it.

At last, in response to the familiar empty feeling in his belly, Diddy went down the hill. He ate breakfast in a little "Instant" restaurant. And then, happy, he caught a helicar and headed for home.

In the master bedroom, Craig heard the outer door of the apartment open—and almost he was too slow. He caught his wife with her fingers on the knob of the door.

He shook his head at her gently. "He'll be tired." he said softly. "Let him rest."

Reluctantly, she allowed herself to be led back, to her own bed this time.

Diddy tiptoed across the living-room to the Play Square and undressed. As he crept under the sheets, he grew aware of the faint tremor of the air. Lying there, he felt the quaver of his bed and heard the shudder of the plexiglas windows. Below him, the floor creaked ever so faintly in its remote, never-ending rapport with the all-pervading vibration.

Diddy grinned happily, but with a great weariness. He'd never have to wonder about the sound again. It was a miasm of the Yards, a thin smoke of vibration from the masses of buildings and metal and machines that tendriled out from the "Way." That sound would be with him all his life; for when the ship was finished, a similar, pervasive sound would shake from every metal plate.

He slept, feeling the pulse of the sound deep inside him, a part of his life.

Completing him.

the search

THE hospital bed was hard under his body. For a moment it seemed to Drake that that was what was bothering him. He turned over into a more comfortable position, and knew it wasn't physical at all. It was something in his mind, the sense of emptiness that had been there since they had told him the date.

After what seemed a long time, the door opened, and two men and a nurse came in. One of the men said in a hearty voice. "Well, how are you, Drake? It's a shame to see you down like this."

The man was plumpish, a good-fellow type. Drake took his vigorous handshake, lay very still for a moment, and then allowed the awkward but very necessary question to escape his lips. "I'm sorry," he said stiffly, "but do I know you?"

The man said, "I'm Bryson, sales manager of the Quik-Rite Company. We manufacture fountain pens, pencils, ink, writing paper, and a dozen kindred lines that even grocery stores handle. Two weeks ago, I hired you and put you on the road as salesman. The next thing I knew you were found unconscious in a ditch, and the hospital advised me you were here." He finished, "You had identification papers on you connecting you with us."

Drake nodded. But he was disappointed. He had thought it would be enough to have someone fill a gap in his mind. It wasn't. He said finally, "My last remembrance is my decision to apply for a job with your firm, Mr. Bryson. I had just been turned down by the draft board for an odd reason. Apparently, something happened to my mind at that point and—"

He stopped. His eyes widened at the thought that came. He said slowly, conscious of an unpleasant sensation, "Apparently, I've had amnesia."

He saw that the house doctor, who had come in with Bryson, was looking at him sharply. Drake mustered a wan

146

smile. "I guess it's all right, doc. What gets me is the kind of life I must have lived these last two weeks. I've been lying here straining my brain. There's something in the back of my mind, but I can't remember what."

The doctor was smiling behind his *pince-nez*. "I'm glad you're taking it so well. Nothing to worry about, really. As for what you did, I assure you that our experience has been that the victim usually lives a reasonably normal life. One of the most frequent characteristics is that the victim of amnesia takes up a different occupation. You didn't even do that."

He paused, and the plump Bryson said heartily, "I can clear up the first week for you. I had discovered, when I hired you, that you'd lived as a boy in some village on the Warwick Junction-Kissling branch line. Naturally, I put you on that route.

"We had orders from you from five towns on the way, but you never got to Kissling. Maybe that will help you . . . No!" Bryson shrugged. "Well, never mind. As soon as you're up, Drake, come and see me. You're a good man, and they're getting scarce."

Drake said, "I'd like to be on the same territory, if it's all right."

Bryson nodded. "Mind you, it's only a matter of finishing up what you missed before, and then moving farther along the main line. But it's yours, certainly. I guess you want to check up on what happened to you."

"That," said Drake, "is exactly what I have in mind. Sort of a search for my memory." He managed a smile. "But now . . . but now, I want to thank you for coming."

"That's all right. S'long."

Bryson shook hands warmly, and Drake watched him out of the door.

Two days later, Drake climbed off the *Transcontinental* at Warwick junction, and stood blinking in the bright sun of early morning. His first disappointment had already come. He had hoped that the sight of the cluster of houses silhouetted against a line of hills would bring back memories.

It had, but only from his boyhood when he and his parents had passed through the Junction on various trips. There were new houses now, and a railway station that hadn't been there twenty years before. Too obviously his mind was not being jarred into the faintest remembrance of what he had done or seen sixteen days earlier. Drake shook his head in bewilderment. "Somebody knew me," he thought. "Somebody must have seen me. I talked to storekeepers, travelers, trainmen, hotel men. I've always had a sociable bent, so—"

"Hello, there Drake, old chap," said a cheerful voice beside him. "You look as if you're thinking about a funeral."

Drake turned, and saw a rather slender young man, dark-faced and dark-haired, about thirty years old. He had the slouch of a too-thin person who had carried too many sample cases. He must have noticed something in Drake's eyes for he said quickly:

"You remember me, don't you? Bill Kellie!" He laughed easily. "Say, come to think of it, I've got a bone to pick with you. What did you do with that girl, Selanie? I've been twice past Piffer's Road since I last saw you, and she didn't come around either time. She—" He stopped, and his gaze was suddenly sharp. "Say, you do remember me, don't you?"

To Drake, the astounding if not notable fact was that Piffer's Road should be the place name. Was it possible that he had got the idea of going to the farmhouse where he had been born, to look the old homestead over. He emerged from his intense inner excitement, and realized from the expression on Kellie's face that it was time to explain. He did so, finishing finally, "So you see, I'm in quite a mental fix. Maybe, if you don't mind, you could give me some idea of what happened while I was with you. Who is this girl, Selanie?"

"Oh, sure," said Kellie, "sure I'll—" He paused, frowned. "You're not kidding me, are you?" He waved Drake silent. "O.K., O.K., I'll believe you. We've got a half-hour before the Kissling local is due. Amnesia, eh? I've heard about that stuff, but sa-a-ay, you don't think that old man could have anything to do with—" He banged his right fist into his left palm. "I'll bet that's it."

"An old man!" Drake said. He caught himself, finished firmly, "What about this story?"

The train slowed. Through the streaky window, Drake could see a rolling valley with patches of green trees and a gleaming, winding thread of water. Then some houses came into view, half a dozen siding tracks, and finally the beginning of a wooden platform.

A tall, slim, fine-looking girl walked past his window carrying a basket. Behind Drake the traveling salesman who had got on at the last stop and to whom he had been talking said, "Oh, there's Selanie. I wonder what kind of supergadget she's got for sale today."

Drake leaned back in his seat, conscious that he had seen all of Piffer's Road that he cared to. It was queer, that feeling of disinterest. After all, he had been born three miles along the road. Nevertheless, there it was. He didn't give a darn. His mind fastened only slowly on what the other had said. "Selanie!" he echoed then. "Curious name! Did you say she sells things?"

"*Does* she sell things!" Kellie spoke explosively.

He must have realized the forcefulness of his words, for he drew a deep, audible breath. His blue eyes looked hard at Drake. He started to say something, stopped himself, and finally sat smiling a secret smile. After a moment, he said, "You know, I really must apologize. I've just now realized that I've monopolized the conversation ever since we started talking."

Drake smiled with polite tolerance. "You've been very entertaining."

Kellie persisted, "What I mean by this is, it's just penetrated to me that you told me you sold fountain pens, among other things."

Drake shrugged. He wondered if he looked as puzzled as he was beginning to feel. He watched as Kellie drew out a pen and held it out for him to take. Kellie said, "See anything odd about that?"

The pen was long, slender, of a dark, expensive-looking material. Drake unscrewed the cap slowly—slowly, because in his mind was the sudden, wry thought that he was in for one of those pointless arguments about the relative merits of the pens he was selling. He said quickly, "This looks right out of my class. My company's pens retail for a dollar."

The moment he had spoken, he realized he had left himself wide open. Kellie said with a casual triumph, "That's exactly what she charged me for it."

"Who?"

"Selanie! The girl who just got on the train. She'll be along in a few minutes selling something new. She's always got an item that's new and different."

He grabbed the pen from Drake's fingers. "I'll show you what's queer about this pen." He reached for a paper cup that stood on the window sill. He said with irritating smugness, "Watch!"

The pen tilted over the cup; Kellie seemed to press with his fingers on the top. Ink began to flow.

After about three minutes, it filled the cup to the brim. Kellie opened the window, carefully emptied the blue liquid on to the ground between the coach and the platform. Drake erupted from his paralysis.

"Good heavens!" he gasped. "What kind of a tank have you got inside that pen? Why, it—"

"Wait!"

Kellie's voice was quiet, but he was so obviously enjoying himself that Drake pulled himself together with a distinct effort. His brain began to whirl once more, as Kellie pressed the top again and once again ink began to flow from the fantastic pen. Kellie said, "Notice anything odd about that ink?"

Drake started to shake his head, then he started to say that the oddness was the quantity, then he gulped hoarsely, "*Red* ink!"

"Or maybe," Kellie said coolly, "you'd prefer purple. Or yellow. Or green. Or violet."

The pen squirted a tiny stream of each color, as he named it. In each case, he turned the part he was pressing ever so slightly. Kellie finished with the triumphant tone of a man who had extracted every last drop of drama from a situation, "Here, maybe you'd like to try it yourself."

Drake took the remarkable thing like a connoisseur caressing a priceless jewel. As from a great distance he heard Kellie chattering on. "—her father makes them," Kellie was saying. "He's a genius with gadgets. You ought to see some of the stuff she's been selling on this train the last month. One of these days he's going to get wise to himself and start large-scale manufacture. When that day comes, all fountain pen companies and a lot of other firms go out of business."

It was a thought that had already occurred to Drake. Before he could muster his mind for speech, the pen was taken from his fingers, and Kellie was leaning across the aisle toward a handsome gray-haired man who sat there. Kellie said, "I noticed you looking at the pen, sir, while I was showing it to my friend. Would you like to examine it?"

"Why, yes," said the man.

He spoke in a low tone, but the sound had a resonance that tingled in Drake's ears. The old man's fingers grasped the extended pen and, just like that, the pen broke.

"Oh!" Kellie exclaimed blankly.

"I beg your pardon," said the fine-looking old man. A dollar appeared in his hand. "My fault. You can buy another one from the girl when she comes." He leaned back, and buried himself behind a newspaper.

Drake saw that Kellie was biting his lip. The man sat staring at his broken pen, and then at the dollar bill, and then in the direction of the now hidden face of the gray-haired man. At last, Kellie sighed. "I can't understand it. I've had the pen a month. It's already fallen to a concrete sidewalk, and twice on to a hardwood floor—and now it breaks like a piece of rotted wood." He shrugged, but his tone was complaining as he went on after a moment, "I suppose actually you can't really expect Selanie's father to do a first-rate job with the facilities he's got—" He broke off excitedly, "Oh, look, there's Selanie now. I wonder what she's featuring today." A sly smile crept into his narrow face. "Just wait till I confront her with that broken pen. I kidded her when I bought it, told her there must be a trick to it. She got mad then, and guaranteed it for life—what the devil is she selling, anyway? Look, they're crowding around her."

Drake climbed to his feet. He craned his neck the better to see over the heads of the crowd that was watching the girl demonstrate something at the far end of the car.

"Good heavens!" a man's deep voice exclaimed. "How much are you charging for those cups? How do they work?"

"Cups!" said Drake, and moved toward the group in a haze of fascination. If he had seen right, the girl was handing around a container which kept filling full of liquid. And people would drink, and it would fill again instantly. Drake thought: The same principle as the fountain pen. Somehow, her father had learned to precipitate liquids. There was genius here. And if he could make a deal with the man for the company, or for himself, he was made.

The tremendous thought ended, as the girl's crystal-clear voice rose above the excited babble, "The price is one dollar each. It works by chemical condensation of gases in the air.

The process is known only to my father. But wait, I haven't finished my demonstration."

She went on, her voice cool and strong against the silence that settled around her, "As you see, it's a folding drinking cup without a handle. First, you open it. Then you turn the top strip clockwise. At a certain point, water comes. But now—watch. I'm turning it further. The liquid is now turning green, and is a sweet and very flavorsome drink. I turn the strip still further, and the liquid turns red, becomes a sweet-sourish drink that is very refreshing in hot weather."

She handed the cup around. While it was being passed from fingers to clutching fingers, Drake managed to wrench his gaze from the gadget, and really look at the girl. She was tall, about five feet six, and she had dark-brown hair. Her face was unmistakably of a fine intelligence. It was thin and good-looking, and there was an odd proud tilt to it that gave her a startling appearance of aloofness in spite of the way she was taking the dollar bills that were being thrust at her.

Once again, her voice rose, "I'm sorry, only one to a person. They'll be on the general market right after the war. These are only souvenirs."

The crowd dissolved, each person retiring to his or her individual seat. The girl came along the aisle, and stopped in front of Drake. He stepped aside instinctively, realized what he was doing, and said piercingly, "Wait! My friend showed me a fountain pen you were selling. I wonder—"

"I still have a few." She nodded gravely. "Would you like a cup, also?"

Drake reminded Kellie. "My friend would like another pen, too. His broke and—"

"I'm sorry, I can't sell him a second pen." She paused. Her eyes widened. She said with a weighty slowness. "Did you say—*his* broke?"

Astoundingly, she swayed. She said wildly, "Let me see that! Where is your friend?"

She took the two pieces of fountain pen from Kellie's fingers, and stared at them. Her mouth began to tremble. Her hands shook. Her face took on a gray, drawn look. Her voice, when she spoke, was a whisper. "Tell me . . . how did it happen? *Exactly* how?"

"Why—"—Kellie drew back in surprise—"I was handing it to that old gentleman over there when—"

He stopped because he had lost his audience. The girl spun on her heel. It was like a signal. The old man lowered his paper, and looked at her. She stared back at him with the fascinated expression of a bird cornered by a snake. Then, for a second time within two minutes, she swayed. The basket nearly dropped from her hand as she ran, but somehow she hung on to it, as she careened along the aisle.

A moment later, Drake saw her racing across the platform. She became a distant, running form on Piffer's Road.

"What the hell!" Kellie exploded.

He whirled on the old man. "What did you do to her?" he demanded fiercely. "You—"

His voice sank into silence, and Drake, who had been about to add his hard words to the demand, remained quiet, also.

The salesman's voice there under the bright sun on the platform at Warwick Junction faded. It required a moment for Drake to grasp that the story was finished.

"You mean," he demanded, "that's all? We just sat there like a couple of dummies, out-faced by an old man? And that was the end of the business? You still don't know what scared the girl?"

He saw there was, on Kellie's face, the strange look of a man who was searching mentally for a word or phrase to describe the indescribable. Kellie said finally:

"There was something about him like . . . like all the tough sales managers in the world rolled into one, and feeling their orneriest. We just shut up."

It was a description that Drake could appreciate. He nodded grimly, said slowly, "He didn't get off?"

"No, you were the only one who got off."

"Eh?"

Kellie looked at him. "You know, this is the damnedest, funniest thing. But that's the way it was. You asked the trainman to check your bags at Inchney. The last thing I saw of you before the train pulled out, you were walking up Piffer's Road in the direction the girl had gone and—Ah, here comes the Kissling local now."

The combination freight and passenger train backed in noisily. Later, as it was winding in and out along the edge of a valley, Drake sat staring wonderingly at the terrain so dimly remembered from his boyhood, only vaguely conscious of Kellie chattering beside him. He decided finally on the course he would take: this afternoon he'd get off at Inchney, make his rounds until the stores closed, then get a ride in some way to Piffer's Road and spend the long, summer evening making inquiries. If he recollected correctly, the distance between the large town and the tiny community was given as seven miles. At worst he could walk back to Inchney in a couple of hours.

The first part proved even simpler than that. There was a bus, the clerk at the Inchney Hotel told him, that left at six o'clock.

At twenty after six, Drake climbed off and, standing in the dirt that was Piffer's Road, watched the bus throb off down the highway. The sound faded into remoteness as he trudged across the railway track. The evening was warm and quiet, and his coat made a weight on his arm. It would be cooler later on, he thought, but at the moment he almost regretted he had brought it.

There was a woman on her knees, working on the lawn at the first house. Drake hesitated, then went over to the fence and stared at the woman for a moment. He wondered if he ought to remember her. He said finally, "I beg your pardon, madam."

She did not look up. She did not rise from the flower-bed, where she was digging. She was a bony creature in a print dress, and she must have seen him coming to be so obstinately silent. "I wonder," Drake persisted, "if you can tell me where a middle-aged man and his daughter live. The daughter is called Selanie, and she used to sell fountain pens and drinking cups and things to people on the train."

The woman was getting up. She came over. At close range, she didn't seem quite so large or ungainly. She had gray eyes that looked at him with a measure of hostility, then with curiosity. "Sa-a-ay," she said sharply, "weren't you along here about two weeks ago asking about them? I told you then that they lived in that grove over there." She waved at some trees about a quarter of a mile along the road, but her eyes were narrowed as she stared at him. "I don't get it," she said grimly.

Drake couldn't see himself explaining about his amnesia to this crusty-voiced, suspicious creature, and he certainly wasn't going to mention that he had once lived in the district. He said hastily, "Thank you very much. I—"

"No use you going up there again," said the woman. "They pulled out on the same day you were there last time ... in their big trailer. And they haven't come back."

"They're gone!" Drake exclaimed.

In the intensity of his disappointment he was about to say more. Then he saw that the woman was staring at him with a faint, satisfied smile on her face. She looked as if she had successfully delivered a knock-out blow to an unpleasant individual. "I think," Drake snapped, "I'll go up and have a look around, anyway."

He spun on his heel, so angry that for a while he scarcely realized that he was walking in the ditch and not on the road. His fury yielded slowly to disappointment, and that in turn faded before the thought that, now that he was up here, he *might* as well have a look.

After a moment, he felt amazed that he could have let one woman get on his nerves to such an extent in so short a time. He shook his head, self-chidingly. He'd better be careful. The process of tracking down his memory was wearing on him.

A breeze sprang up from nowhere as he turned into the shadowed grove. It blew softly in his face, and its passage through the trees was the only sound that broke the silence of the evening. It didn't take more than a moment to realize that his vague expectations, the sense of—something—that had been driving him on to this journey was not going to be satisfied. For there was nothing, not a sign that human beings had ever lived here; not a tin can, or a bundle of garbage, or ashes from a stove. Nothing. He wandered around disconsolately for a few minutes, poked gingerly with a stick among a pile of dead branches. And finally, he walked back along the road. This time it was the woman who called to him. He hesitated, then went over. After all, she might know a lot more than she had told. He saw that she looked more friendly.

"Find anything?" she said with an ill-restrained eagerness.

Drake smiled grimly at the power of curiosity, then shrugged ruefully. "When a trailer leaves," he said, "it's like smoke—it just vanishes."

The woman sniffed. "Any traces that were left sure went fast after the old man got through there."

Drake fought to hold down his excitement. "The old man!" he exclaimed.

The woman nodded, then said bitterly, "A fine looking old fellow. Came around first inquiring from everybody what kind of stuff Selanie had sold us. Two days later, we woke up in the morning, and every single piece was gone."

"Stolen!"

The woman scowled. "Same thing as. There was a dollar bill for each item. But that's stealing for those kind of goods. Do you know, she had a frying pan that—"

"But what did he want?" Drake interrupted, bewildered. "Didn't he explain anything when he was making his inquiries? Surely, you didn't just let him come around here asking questions!"

To his astonishment the woman grew flustered. "I don't know what came over me," she confessed finally, sullenly. "There was something about him. He looked kind of commanding-like and important, as if he were a big executive or something." She stopped angrily. "The scoundrel!" she snapped.

Her eyes narrowed with abrupt hostility. She peered at Drake. "You're a fine one for saying did he ask any questions. What about you? Standing here pumping me when all the time—Say, let me get this straight: *Are* you the fellow who called here two weeks ago? Just how do you fit into the picture?"

Drake hesitated. The prospect of having to tell that story to people like this seemed full of difficulties. And yet, she must know more. There must be a great deal of information about the month that the girl Selanie and her father spent in the district. One thing seemed certain. If any more facts were available, this woman would have them.

His hesitation ended. He made his explanation, but finished a little uncertainly: "So you see, I'm a man who is—well—in search of his memory. Maybe I was knocked over the head, although there's no lump. Then, again, maybe I was doped. *Something* happened to me. You say I went up there. Did I come back? Or what did I do?"

He stopped with a jump, for, without warning, the woman parted her lips and let out a bellow. "*Jimmy!*" she yelled in an ear-splitting voice, "Jimmy! *C'm'ere!*"

"Yeah, mum!" came a boy's voice from inside the house.

Drake stared blankly as an uncombed twelve-year-old with a sharp, eager face, catapulted out of the house. The screen door banged behind him. Drake listened, still with only partial comprehension, as the mother explained to the boy that "this man was hit over the head by those people in the trailer, and he lost his memory, and he'd like you to tell him what you saw."

The woman turned to Drake. "Jimmy," she said proudly, "never trusted those folk. He was sure they were foreigners or something, and so he kept a sharp eye on them. He saw you go up there, and everything that happened right up to the time the trailer left." She finished. "The reason he can tell you in such detail exactly what you did is that he could see everything through the windows, and besides, he went inside once when they weren't around and looked the whole place over, just to make sure, of course, that they weren't pulling something."

Drake nodded, suppressing his cynicism. It was probably as good a reason as any for snooping. In this case, it was lucky for him.

The thought ended, as Jimmy's shrill voice projected into the gathering twilight.

The afternoon was hot. Drake, after pausing to inquire of the woman in the first house as to where the father and daughter lived, walked slowly toward the grove of trees she had indicated.

Behind him, the train tooted twice, and then began to chuff. Drake suppressed a startled impulse to run back and get on it. He realized he couldn't have made it, anyway. Besides, a man didn't give up hope of fortune as easily as that. His pace quickened as he thought of the pen and the drinking cup.

He couldn't see the trailer in the grove until he turned into the initial shady patch of trees. When he saw it, he stopped short. It was much bigger than he had conceived it. It was as long as a small freight car, and as big, curiously streamlined.

No one answered his knock.

He thought tensely: She ran this way. She must be inside. Uncertain, he walked around the monster on wheels. There was a line of windows above the level of his eyes that made a complete circuit of the trailer. He could see a gleamy ceiling and the upper part of what looked like finely paneled walls. There were three rooms, and the only other entrance led into the cab of the truck to which the trailer was attached.

Back before the first entrance, Drake listened intently for sounds. But again there was nothing—nothing except a thin wind that blew gently through the upper reaches of the trees. Far away, the train whistled plaintively. He tried the latch, and the door opened so easily that his hesitation ended. Deliberately, he pushed it ajar, and stood there staring into the middle room of the three.

His startled gaze met luxury. The floor was a marvel, a darkly gleaming, gemlike design. The walls toned in with an amazingly rich-looking, though quiet, panel effect. There was a couch just across from the door, two chairs, three cabinets, and several intricately carved shelves with art objects standing on them. The first thing Drake saw, as he climbed in, was the girl's basket standing against the wall just to the left of the door.

The sight stopped him short. He sat in the doorway, then, his legs dangling toward the ground. His nervousness yielded to the continuing silence and he began with a developing curiosity to examine the contents of the basket. There were about a dozen of the magic pens, at least three dozen of the folding, self-filling cups, a dozen roundish black objects that refused to respond to his handling, and three pairs of *pince-nez* glasses. Each pair had a tiny, transparent wheel attached to the side of the right lens. They seemed to have no cases; there seemed to be no fear that they would break. The pair he tried on fitted snugly over his nose, and for a moment he actually thought they fitted his eyes. Then he noticed the difference. Everything was nearer—the room, his hand—not magnified or blurred, but it was as if he were gazing through mildly powered field glasses. There was no strain on his eyes. After a moment, he grew conscious again of the little wheel. It turned quite easily.

Instantly, things were nearer, the field-glass effect twice as strong. Trembling a little, he began to turn the wheel, first one way, then the other. A few seconds only were needed to verify the remarkable reality. He had on a pair of *pince-nez* with adjustable lenses, an incredible combination of telescope-microscope: superglasses.

Almost blankly, Drake returned the marvelous things to

the basket and with abrupt decision, climbed into the trailer and moved toward the entrance to the back room. His intention was to glance in only. But that first look showed the entire wall fitted with shelves, each neatly loaded with a variety of small goods. Drake picked up what looked like a camera. It was a finely made little instrument. He studied the lens; his fingers pressed something that gave. There was a click. Instantly, a glistening card came out of a slit in the back. A picture.

It was of the upper part of a man's face. It had remarkable depth and an amazing natural color effect. It was the intent expression in the brown eyes that momentarily made the features unfamiliar. Then he recognized that he was looking at himself. He had taken his picture, and instantly it had been developed.

Astounded, Drake stuffed the picture in his pocket, set the instrument down, and, trembling, climbed out of the trailer and walked off down the road toward the village.

"—and then," said Jimmy, "a minute later you came back and climbed in and shut the door and went into the back room. You came back so fast that you nearly saw me; I thought you'd gone. And then—"

The trailer door opened. A girl's voice said something urgent that Drake didn't catch. The next instant, a man answered with a grunt. The door closed; and there was a movement and the sound of breathing in the center room.

Crouching, Drake drew back against the left wall.

"—and that's all, mister," Jimmy finished. "I thought there was going to be trouble then. And I hiked for home to tell mum."

"You mean," Drake protested, "I was foolish enough to come back just in time to get myself caught, and I didn't dare show myself?"

The boy shrugged. "You were pressing up against the partition. That's all I could see."

"And they didn't look in that room while you were watching?"

Jimmy hesitated. "Well," he began finally in a curious, defensive tone, "what happened then was kind of queer. You see, I looked back when I'd gone about a hundred yards, and the trailer and truck wasn't there no more."

"Wasn't there?" Drake spoke slowly. He had a sense of unreality. "You mean, they started up the truck engine, and drove to Piffer's Road, and so on down to the highway?"

The boy shook his head stubbornly. "Folks is always trying to trip me up on that. But I know what I saw and heard. There weren't no sound of an engine. They just was gone suddenly, that's all."

Drake felt an eerie chill along his spine. "And I was aboard?" he asked.

"You was aboard," said Jimmy.

The silence that followed was broken by the woman saying loudly, "All right, Jimmy, you can go and play."

She turned back to Drake. "Do you know what I think?" she said.

With an effort, Drake roused himself. "What?" he said.

"They're working a racket, the whole bunch of them together. The story about her father making the stuff. I can't understand how we fell for that. He just spent his time going around the district buying up old metal. Mind you"—the admission came almost reluctantly—"they've got some wonderful things. The government isn't kidding when it says that after this war we're going to live like kings and queens. But there's the rub. So far, these people have only got hold of a few hundred pieces altogether. What they do is sell them in one district, then steal back and resell in another."

In spite of his intense self-absorption, Drake stared at her. He had run across the peculiar logic of fuzzy-minded people before, but it always shocked him when facts were so brazenly ignored in order that a crackpot theory might hold water. He said, "I don't see where the profit comes in. What about the dollar you got back for each item that was stolen?"

"Oh!" said the woman. Her face lengthened. Then she looked startled. And then, as she grasped how completely her pet idea was wrecked, an angry flush suffused her wind-and-sun-tanned face. "Some publicity scheme, maybe!" she snapped.

It struck Drake that it was time to terminate the interview. He said hastily, "Is anyone you know going into Inchney tonight? I'd like a ride if I could get it."

The change of subject did its work. The high color faded from the woman's cheeks. She said thoughtfully:

"Nope, no one I know of. But don't worry. Just get on the highway, and you'll get a lift—"

The second car picked him up. He sat in the hotel, as darkness fell, thinking: "A girl and her father with a carload of the finest manufactured goods in the world. She sells them as souvenirs, one to a person. He buys old metal. And then, as added insanity, an old man goes around buying up the goods sold"—he thought of Kellie's pen—"or breaking them." Finally, there was the curious amnesia of a fountain-pen salesman, named Drake.

Somewhere behind Drake, a man's voice cried out in anguish, "Oh, look what you've done now. You've broken it."

A quiet, mature, resonant voice answered, "I beg your pardon. You paid a dollar for it, you say? I shall pay for the loss, naturally. Here—and you have my regrets."

In the silence that followed, Drake stood up and turned. He saw a tall, splendid-looking man with gray hair, in the act of rising from beside a younger chap who was staring at the two pieces of a broken pen in his fingers. The old man headed for the revolving door leading to the street, but it was Drake who got there first, Drake who said quietly but curtly, "One minute, please. I want an explanation of what happened to me after I got into the trailer of the girl, Selanie, and her father. And I think you're the man to give it to me."

He stopped. He was staring into eyes that were like pools of gray fire, eyes that seemed literally to tear into his face, and to peer with undiminished intensity at the inside of his brain. Drake had time for a brief, startled memory of what Kellie had said about the way this man had outfaced them on the train with one deadly look, and then it was too late for further thought. With a tigerish speed, the other stepped forward and caught Drake's wrist. There was the feel of metal in that touch, metal that sent a tingling glow along Drake's arm, as the old man said in a low, compelling voice, "This way—to my car."

Barely, Drake remembered getting into a long, gleamy-hooded car. The rest was darkness—mental—physical—

He was lying on his back on a hard floor. Drake opened his eyes and for a blank moment stared at a domed ceiling two hundred feet above him. The ceiling was at least three hundred feet wide, and nearly a quarter of it was window, through which a gray white mist of light showed, as if an invisible sun were trying hard to penetrate a thin but persistent fog.

The wide strip of window ran along the center of the ceiling straight on into the distance. Into the *distance!* With a gasp, Drake jerked erect. For a moment then his mind wouldn't accept what his eyes saw.

There was no end to that corridor. It stretched in either direction until it became a blur of gray marble and gray light. There was a balcony and a gallery and a second gallery; each floor had its own side corridor, set off by a railing. And there were countless shining doors and, every little while, a branch corridor, each suggesting other vast reaches of that visibly monstrous building.

Very slowly, the first enormous shock over, Drake climbed to his feet. Memory of the old man—and what had gone before—was a weight in his mind. He thought darkly: "He got me into his car, and drove me here."

But why was he here? On all the wide surface of the Earth, no such building existed.

A chill went up his spine. It cost him a distinct effort to walk toward the nearest of the long line of tall, carved doors, and pull it open. What he expected, he couldn't have told. But his first reaction was disappointment. It was an office, a large room with plain walls. There were some fine-looking cabinets along one wall. A great desk occupied the corner facing the door. Some chairs and two comfortable-looking settees and another, more ornate door completed the picture. No one was in the room. The desk looked spick and span, dustless. And lifeless.

The other door proved to be locked, or else the catch was too complicated for him to work.

Out in the corridor again, Drake grew conscious of the intense silence. His shoes clicked with an empty sound. And door after door yielded the same office-furnished but uninhabited interior.

Half an hour passed, by his watch. And then another half-hour. And then he saw the door in the distance. At first it was only a brightness. It took on glittering contours, became an enormous glass affair set in a framework of multi-tinted windows. The door was easily fifty feet in height. When he peered through its transparent panes, he could see great white steps leading down into a mist that thickened after about twenty feet, so that the lower steps were not visible.

Drake stared uneasily. There was something wrong here. That mist, obscuring everything, persisting for hours, clinging darkly. He shook himself. Probably there was water down there at the foot of the steps, warmish water subjected to a constant stream of cold air, and thick fog formed. He pictured that in his mind, a building ten miles long standing beside a lake, and buried forever in gray mists.

"Get out of here," Drake thought sharply.

The latch of the door was at a normal height. But it was hard to believe that he would be able to maneuver the gigantic structure with such a comparatively tiny leverage. It opened lightly, gently, like a superbly balanced machine. Drake stepped out into the pressing fog and began, swiftly at first, and then with a developing caution, to go down the steps. No use landing up in a pool of deep water. The hundredth step was the last; and there was no water. There was nothing except mists, no foundations for the steps, no ground.

On hands and knees, dizzy with a sudden vertigo, Drake crawled back up the steps. He was so weak that inches only seemed to recede behind him. The nightmarish feeling came that the steps were going to crumble under him, now that he had discovered that their base was—nothing.

A second, greater fear came that the door would not open from the outside, and he would be cut off here, on the edge of eternity, forever. But it did open. It took all the strength of his weakened body. He lay on the floor inside, and after a while the awful wonder came to his mind: What did a girl called Selanie, dispensing marvelous gadgets on a train, have to do with this? There seemed to be no answer.

His funk yielded to the sense of safety produced by the passing minutes. He stood up, ashamed of his terror, and his mind grooving to a purpose. He must explore the fantastic place from cellar to roof. Somewhere, there would be a cache of the cups that created their own water. And perhaps also there would be food. Soon, he would have to eat and drink. But first, to one of the offices. Examine every cabinet, break open the desk drawers and search them.

It wasn't necessary to break anything. The drawers opened at the slightest tug. The cabinet doors were unlocked. Inside were journals, ledgers, curious looking files. Absorbed,

Drake glanced blurrily through several that he had spread out on the great desk, blurrily because his hands were shaking and his brain seemed to be jumping. Finally, with an effort of will, he pushed everything aside but one of the journals. This he opened at random, and read the words printed there:

SYNOPSIS OF REPORT OF POSSESSOR KINGSTON CRAIG IN THE MATTER OF THE EMPIRE OF LYCEUS II A.D. 27,346-27,378

Frowning, Drake stared at the date; then he read on:

The normal history of the period is a tale of cunning usurpation of power by a ruthless ruler. A careful study of the man revealed an unnatural urge to protect himself at the expense of others.

TEMPORARY SOLUTION: A warning to the Emperor, who nearly collapsed when he realized that he was confronted by a Possessor. His instinct for self-preservation impelled him to give guarantees as to future conduct.

COMMENT: This solution produced a probability world Type 5, and must be considered temporary because of the very involved permanent work that Professor Link is doing on the fringes of the entire two hundred and seventy-third century.

CONCLUSION: Returned to the Palace of Immortality after an absence of three days.

Drake sat there stiffly, at first, then he leaned back in his chair; but the same blank impression remained in his mind. There seemed to be nothing to think about the report. At last, he turned a leaf, and read:

SYNOPSIS OF REPORT OF POSSESSOR KINGSTON CRAIG

This is the case of Laird Graynon, Police inspector, 900th Sector Station, New York City, who on July 7, A.D. 2830, was falsely convicted of accepting bribes, and de-energized.

SOLUTION: Obtained the retirement of Inspector Graynon two months before the date given in the charge. He retired to his farm, and henceforth exerted the very minimum of influence on the larger scene of existence. He lived in this probability world of his own until his death in 2874, and thus provided an almost perfect 290A.

CONCLUSION: Returned to the Palace of Immortality after one hour.

There were more entries, hundreds—thousands altogether in the several journals. Each one was a "REPORT OF POSSESSOR KINGSTON CRAIG", and always he returned to the "Palace of Immortality" after so many days, or hours, or weeks. Once it was three months, and that was an obscure, impersonal affair that dealt with the "establishment of the time of demarcation between the ninety-eighth and ninety-ninth centuries—" and involved "the resurrection into active, personal probability worlds of their own of three murdered men, named—"

The sharpening pangs of thirst and hunger brought to Drake a picture of himself sitting in this immense and terrible building, reading the fanciful scrawlings of a man who *must* be mad. It struck him that the seemingly resourceless light of the room was growing dimmer. The light must come in some way from outside. Out in the vast, empty corridor, he realized the truth. The mists above the ceiling window were graying, darkening. Night was falling. He tried not to think of that, of being alone in this tomblike building, watching the gloom creep over the gray marble, wondering what things might come out of hiding once the darkness grew impenetrable.

"Stop it, you fool!" Drake said aloud, savagely.

His voice sounded hollow against the silence. He thought: There must be a place here where these—Possessors—had lived. This floor was all offices, but there were other floors. He must find a stairway. He had seen none on the main corridor.

He found one fifty feet along the first side corridor. A broad staircase. Drake bounded up the steps and tried the first door he came to. It opened into the living-room of a magnificent apartment. There were seven rooms, including a kitchen that gleamed in the dimming light, and the built-in cupboards of which were packed with transparent containers. The contents were foods both familiar and strange.

Drake felt without emotion. Nor was he surprised as he manipulated a tiny lever at the top of a can of pears and the fruit spilled out on to the table, although the can had not opened in any way. He saw to it that he had a dish for the next attempt; that was all. Later, after he had eaten, he searched for light switches. But it was becoming too dark to see.

The main bedroom had a canopied bed that loomed in the darkness, and there were pajamas in a drawer. Lying between the cool sheets, his body heavy with approaching sleep, Drake thought vaguely: That girl Selanie and her fear of the old man—why had she been afraid. And what *could* have happened in the trailer that has irrevocably precipitated Ralph Carson Drake into this?

He slept uneasily, with the thought still in his mind.

The light was far away at first. It came nearer, grew brighter, and at first it was like any awakening. Then, just as Drake opened his eyes, memories flooded his mind. He was lying, he saw tensely, on his left side. It was broad daylight. From the corners of his eyes he could see, above him, the silvery-blue canopy of the bed. Beyond it, far above, was the high ceiling.

In the shadows of the previous evening he had scarcely noticed how big and roomy and luxurious his quarters were. There were thick-piled rugs and paneled walls and rose-colored furniture that glowed with costly beauty. The bed was of oversize four-poster construction.

Drake's thought suffered a dreadful pause because, in turning his head away from the left part of the room toward the right, his gaze fell for the first time on the other half of the bed. A young woman lay there, fast asleep. She had dark-brown hair, a snowy-white throat, and, even in repose, her face looked fine and intelligent. She appeared to be about thirty years old.

Drake's examination got no further. Like a thief in the night, he slid from under the quilt. He reached the floor and crouched there. He held his breath in a desperate dismay as the steady breathing from the bed stopped. There was the sound of a woman sighing, and finally doom!

"My dear," said a rich contralto voice, lazily, "what on earth are you doing on the floor?"

There was movement on the bed, and Drake cringed in anticipation of the scream that would greet the discovery that he was not *the* my dear. But nothing happened. The lovely head came over the edge of the bed. Gray eyes stared at him tranquilly. The young woman seemed to have forgotten her first question, for now she said, "Darling, are you scheduled to go to Earth today?"

That got him. The question itself was so stupendous that his personal relation to everything seemed secondary. Besides, in a dim way he was beginning to understand.

This was one of those worlds of probability that he had read about in the journals of Possessor Kingston Craig. Here was something that *could* happen to Ralph Drake. And somewhere behind the scenes someone was making it happen. All because he had gone in search of his memory.

Drake stood up. He was perspiring. His heart was beating like a trip hammer. His knees trembled. But he stood up, and he said, "Yes, I'm going to Earth."

It gave him purpose, he thought tensely, reason to get out of here as fast as he possibly could. He was heading for the chair on which were his clothes when the import of his own words provided the second and greater shock to his badly shaken system.

Going to Earth! He felt his brain sag before the weight of a fact that trancended every reality of his existence. Going to Earth—from where? The answer was a crazy thing that sighed at last wearily through his mind: From the Palace of Immortality, of course, the palace in the mists, where the Possessors lived.

He reached the bathroom. The night before, he had discovered in its darkening interior a transparent jar of salve, the label of which said: BEARD REMOVER—RUB ON, THEN WASH OFF. It took half a minute; the rest, five minutes longer. He came out of the bathroom, fully dressed. His mind was like a stone in his head, and like a stone sinking through water he started for the door near the bed.

"Darling!"

"Yes?" Cold and stiff, Drake turned. In relief, he saw that she was not looking at him. Instead she had one of the magic pens and was frowning over some figures in a big ledger. Without looking up, she said, "Our time-relation to each other is becoming worse. You'll have to stay more at the palace, reversing your age, while I go to Earth and add a few years to mine. Will you make the arrangements for that dear?"

"Yes," said Drake, "yes!"

He walked into the little hallway, then into the living-room. Out in the corridor at last, he leaned against the cool, smooth marble wall, and thought hopelessly: Reverse his age! So that was what this incredible building did! Every day here you were a day younger, and it was necessary to go to Earth to strike a balance.

The shock grew. Because what had happened to him on the trailer was so important that a super-human organization was striving to prevent him from learning the truth. Somehow, today, he would really have to find out what all this was about, explore every floor, and try to locate some kind of central office. He was relaxing slowly, withdrawing out of that intense inward concentration of his mind when, for the first time, he grew conscious of sounds. Voices, movements, people below him.

Even as he leaped for the balcony balustrade, Drake realized that he should have known. The woman there in the bed—where she had been—had implied a world complete in every detail of life. But he felt shocked, anyway. Bewildered, he stared down at the great main corridor of the building, along the silent, deserted reaches of which he had wandered for so many hours the day before. Now men and women swarmed along it in a steady stream. It was like a city street, with people moving in both directions, all in a hurry, all bent on some private errand.

"Hello, Drake!" said a young man's voice behind him.

Drake had no emotion left for that. He turned slowly, like a tired man. The stranger who stood there regarding him was tall and well-proportioned. He had dark hair and a full, strong face. He wore a shapely one-piece suit, pleasingly form-fitting above the waist. The trouser part puffed out like breeches. He was smiling in a friendly, quizzical fashion. He said finally, coolly:

"So you'd like to know what it's all about? Don't worry, you will. But first, try on this glove, and come with me. My name is Price, by the way."

Drake stared at the extended glove. "What—" he began blankly. He stopped. His mind narrowed around the conviction that he was being rushed along too fast for under-standing. This man waiting for him here at the door was no accident. Drake braced himself. Take it easy, he thought sharply. The overwhelming, important thing was *that* they were out in the open at last. But what about this glove?

He accepted the thing frowning. It was for his right hand. It fitted perfectly. It was light in weight, flexible, but it seemed unnaturally thick. The outer surface had a faint metallic sheen.

"Just grab his shoulder with that glove, from behind," Price was saying. "Press below the collarbone with the points of your fingers, press hard. I'll give you an illustration later, after you've asked any questions you have on your mind."

Before Drake could speak, Price went on, "I'll tell you as we go along. Be careful of those stairs."

Drake caught himself, swallowed hard, and said, "What's all this nonsense about grabbing somebody by the shoulder? Why—"

He stopped hopelessly. That shouldn't be his first question. He was like a blind man being given fragments of information about a world he couldn't see. There was no beginning, no coherence, nothing but these blurry half-facts. He'd have to get back to fundamentals. Ralph Carson Drake was a man in search of his memory. Something had happened to him aboard a trailer, and everything else had followed as the night the day. If he could keep that in mind, he'd be all right.

"Damn you!" Drake said out of the anguish of his bewilderment. "Damn you, Price, I want to know what this is all about."

"Don't get excited." They were down the steps now, heading along the side corridor to the great main hallway. Price half-turned as he spoke. "I know just how you feel, Drake, but you must see that your brain can't be overloaded in one sustained assault of information. Yesterday, you found this place deserted. Well, that wasn't exactly yesterday."

He shrugged. "You see how it is. That was today in the alternative world to this one. That is how this building will be forever if you don't do what we want. We had to show you that. And now, for heaven's sake, don't ask me to explain the science and theory of time-probability."

"Look," said Drake desperately, "let's forget everything else, and concentrate on one fact. You want me to do something with this glove. What? Where? When? Why? I assure you I'm feeling quite reasonable. I—"

His voice faded. He saw suddenly that Price and he were

in the main corridor, heading straight for the great doorway which led to the steps and the misty nothingness beyond them. He had a clammy feeling. He said sharply, "Where are you going?"

"I'm taking you to Earth."

"Out of that door?"

Drake stopped short. He wasn't sure just what he felt, but his voice sounded sharp and tense in his ears.

He saw that Price had paused. The man looked at him steadily. Price said earnestly, "There's nothing strange about any of this, really. The Palace of Immortality was built in an eddy of time, the only known Reverse, or Immortality, Drift in the Earth Time Stream. It has made the work of the Possessors possible, a good work as you know from your reading of Possessor Kingston Craig's reports—" His voice went on, explaining, persuading; but it was hard for Drake to concentrate on his words. That mist bothered him. He couldn't go down those steps again.

It was the word, Possessors, that brought Drake's mind and body back into active operation. He had seen and heard the term so often that for all these long minutes he had forgotten that he didn't know what it meant. He asked, "But who are the Possessors? What do they possess?"

The man looked at him, dark eyes thoughtful. "They possess," he said finally, "the most unique ability ever to distinguish men and women from their fellows. They can go through time at will. There are," Price went on, "about three thousand of them. They were all born over a period of five hundred years beginning in the twentieth century. The strangest thing of all is that every one of them originated in a single, small district of the United States, around the towns of Kissling, Inchney, and particularly in an infinitesimal farming cummunity called Piffer's Road."

"But that," Drake said through dry lips, "is where I was born." His eyes widened. "And that's where the trailer was."

Price seemed not to have heard. "Physically," he said, "the Possessors are also unique. Every one of them has the organs of his or her body the opposite to that of a normal human being. That is, the heart is on the right side and—"

"But I'm like that," Drake said. He spoke precisely, as if he were fumbling his way through a labyrinth. "That's why the draft board rejected me. They said they couldn't take the risk of my getting wounded, because the surgeon wouldn't know my case history."

Behind Drake, footsteps clicked briskly. He turned automatically and stared at the woman in a fluffy, flowing dressing gown who was walking toward them. She smiled as she saw him, the smile he had already seen in the bedroom. She said in her rich voice as she came up:

"Poor fellow! He looks positively ill. Well, I did my best to make the shock easy for him. I gave him as much information as I could without letting on that I knew everything."

Price said, "Oh, he's all right." He turned to Drake. There was a faint smile on his face, as if he were appreciating the situation to the full. "Drake, I want you to meet your wife, formerly Selanie Johns, who will now tell you what happened to you when you climbed aboard her father's trailer at Piffer's Road. Go ahead, Selanie."

Drake stood there. He felt like a clod of earth, empty of emotion and of thought. It was only slowly that he grew aware of her voice telling the story of the trailer.

Standing there in the back room of the trailer, Drake wondered what might happen even now if he should be caught red-handed before he could act. He heard the man in the center room say, "We'll head for the fourteenth century. They don't dare do much monkeying around in this millennium."

He chuckled grimly, "You'll notice that it was the old man they sent, and only one of them at that. Somebody had to go out and spend thirty or forty years growing old, because old men have so much less influence on an environment than young. But we'd better waste no time. Give me those transformer points, and go into the cab and start the atomic transformers."

It was the moment Drake had been waiting for. He stepped out softly, flexing his gloved right hand. He saw the man standing facing in the direction of the door that led to the front room and the engine cab beyond it. From the back, the man looked of stocky build, and about forty-five years of age. In his hands, clutched tight, he held two transparent cones that glowed with a dull light.

"All right," he called gruffly as Drake stepped up behind him. "We're moving. And hereafter, Selanie, don't be so

frightened. The Possessors are through, damn them. I'm sure
our sale of the stuff, and the removal of so much metal has
interfered with the electronic balances that made their existence possible." His voice shook. "When I think of the al-
mighty sacrilege of that outfit, acting like God, daring to use
their powers to change the natural course of existence instead
of, as I suggested, making it a means of historical research—"

His voice collapsed into a startled grunt, as Drake grabbed
his shoulder, and pressed hard below the collarbone—

"—just a minute!" Drake's voice cut piercingly across the
woman's story. "You talk as if I had a glove like this"—he
raised his right hand with its faintly gleaming glove, that
Price had given him—"and there's also a suggestion in your
words that I know everything about the Possessors and the
Palace of Immortality. You're perfectly aware that I knew
nothing at that time. I had just come off a train, where a
fountain pen had been brought to my attention by a salesman
called Bill Kellie."

He saw that the woman was looking at him gravely. She
said, "I'm sure you will understand in a few minutes. Everything that we've done has been designed to lead up to this
moment. Only a few hours of existence remains to this probability world—*this* one, where Mr. Price and you and I are
standing; there is a strange balance of forces involved, and,
paradoxical as it may seem, we are actually working against
time."

Drake stared at her, startled by her tone, as she said urgently: "Let me go on, please—"

The stocky man stood utterly still, like a man who has
been stunned by an intolerable blow. And then, as Drake let
go of his shoulder, he turned slowly, and his gaze fastened
sickly, not on Drake's face, but on the glove he wore.

"A Destroyer glove!" he whispered; then more wildly, "But
how? The repellors are on my special invention that prevents
a trained Possessor coming near me!" he looked for the first
time at Drake's face. "How did you do it? I—"

"Father!" It was the girl's voice, clear and startled, from
the engine cab. Her voice came nearer, "Father, we've
stopped at about A.D. 1650. What's happened? I thought—"

She paused in the doorway like a startled bird, a tall, slim girl around nineteen years, looking suddenly older, grayer, as she saw Drake. "You ... were on ... the ... train!" she said. Her gaze fluttered to her father. She gasped, "Dad, he hasn't—"

The stocky man nodded hopelessly. "He's destroyed my power to go through time. Wherever we are in time and space, we're *there*. Not that that matters. The thing is, we've failed. The Possessors live on to do their work."

The girl said nothing. The two of them seemed totally to have forgotten Drake. The man caught her arm, said hoarsely, "Don't you understand? We failed!"

Still she was silent. Her face had a bleached quality when she answered finally, "Father, this is the hardest thing I've ever said, but I'm glad. *They're* in the right; *you're* wrong. They're trying to do something about the terrible mistakes of Man and Nature. They've made a marvelous science of their great gift, and they use it like beneficent gods. It was easy enough for you to convince me when I was a child, but for years now my doubts have been gathering. I stayed with you through loyalty. I'm sorry father." She turned. There were tears in her eyes as she opened the outer door and jumped to the green ground below.

Drake stood for a moment, fascinated by the play of emotions on the man's face, first a quiver of self-pity, then a gathering over-all expression of obstinacy. A spoiled child couldn't have provided a more enlightening picture of frustrated egoism. One long look Drake took. Then he, too, went to the door. There was the girl to make friends with, and an early western American world to explore and wonder at.

They were thrown into each other's company by the stubborn silence into which the older man retreated. They walked often along the green uninhabited valley, Drake and the girl. Once, a group of Indians on foot confronted the two of them far from the trailer. To Drake it was a question of who was the more startled. Selanie solved the problem with her atomic gun. She fired at a stone. It puffed out of sight in a flare of brilliance. No more Indians ever came that way.

In a way, it was an idyllic life; and love came as easily as the winds that blew mournfully across that lonely land. Came especially because he *knew*, and persisted against her early coldness. After that, they talked more urgently of persuading a self-willed man to train one or the other, or both of them,

how to use their innate ability to travel in time. Drake knew
that the man would give in eventually from sheer loneliness,
but it took a year longer.

Drake's mind drew slowly back into the great domed
palace, and he grew conscious that the woman's voice had
ceased. He stared at her, then at Price. He said finally,
puzzled, "Is that all? Your ... father—" He looked at the
woman, stumbling over the relationship. It was immensely
difficult to connect this mature woman with youthful Selanie
Johns. He pressed on. "You mean, your father was opposed
to the work done by the Possessors? But how did he expect to
eliminate them?"

It was Price who answered, "Mr. Johns' plan was to divert
the local activity that had helped to create the Possessors. We
know that foods definitely played a vital part, but just what
combination of foods and other habits was the root cause, we
have never learned.

"Mr. Johns thought, by having people drink from his cups,
use his other food devices and general articles, he would
break the general pattern of existence away from what it
would normally have followed. His gathering of metal was
also planned. Metal has a very strong influence on the great
Time Stream. Its sudden removal from one time to another
can upset entire worlds of probability. As for us, we could
not interfere, except as you saw. The world prior to the
twenty-fifth century is one age where no work will ever be
done by the Possessors. It must solve its own problems. Even
you, one of the first to possess the gift of time travel, though
you would never of yourself have learned the method, had to
be allowed to move towards your destiny almost naturally."

"Look," said Drake, "either I'm crazy or you are. I'm
willing to accept everything—the existence of this Palace of
Immortality, the fact that she's my wife in some future date,
and that I've sort of dropped in on her before I married her,
but *after* she married me. I'll accept all that, I say, but you
gave me this glove a little while ago, and you said you
wanted me to do something with it, and a few minutes ago
my ... wife ... said that this world was in hourly danger of
being wiped out. Is there something else that you haven't told
me about? And why that spell of amnesia?"

Price cut him off, "Your part in all this is really very

simple. As a salesman of the Quik-Rite Company, you followed Selanie, who was then nineteen years old, to a trailer at Piffer's Road occupied by her father and herself. When you got there, she wasn't to be found, nor was anyone else, so you started back to the village to make inquiries. On the way, however, you were picked up by Possessor Drail McMahon and transported one week ahead in time, and all relevant memory was drained from you. You awakened in the hospital."

"Just a minute!" Drake protested. "My ... wife ... has just told me what else I did. I knew that before, of course. There was an eye witness, a boy named Jimmy, who saw me go back to the trailer, and that I was on it when it disappeared."

"Let me tell you this," Price said coolly. "From the hospital you set out to find what had happened to you. You did find out, and then you were transported here by another Possessor, and here you are."

Drake looked at the man, then at the woman. She nodded, and the first flame was already burning in his mind as Price continued, "In a few moments, I shall take you to Earth to the vicinity of the trailer of Peter Johns and his daughter. You will go aboard, conceal yourself in the back room and at the moment that Selanie has described to you, you will come out and grab her father by the shoulder with the glove. The glove produces energy that will subtly change the potential of his nerve force. It will not harm him, nor will we afterward. As a matter of fact, he will be used as a research agent by us." Price finished simply, "You can see that this action requires free will, and that we had to do everything as we have, to make sure that you would make no mistake."

Drake said, "I can see a lot of things."

He felt himself calm except for the way his soul was expanding. Slowly, he walked over to the woman, took her hand and gazed steadily into her eyes. He said, "This is you—when?"

"Fifty years from now in your life."

"And where am I? Where is your husband?"

"You went to Earth, into the future. You have to be out of the way. The same body cannot be in the same space. And that reminds me. That is the one hold we have on you."

"How?"

"If instead of entering the trailer, you walked off down the road to resume your life, in one week you would reach the time where your earlier self was in hospital. You would vanish, disintegrate."

Drake smiled at her. "I don't think I'm going to muff it," he said.

Looking back, he could see her, as he walked down the steps into the thickening folds of mist. She was standing with her face pressed against the glass of the door.

The mist swallowed her.

His memory search was over. He was about to live the events he thought he had forgotten.